EULOGY FOR THE LIVING

EULOGY FOR THE LIVING

TAKING FLIGHT

Christa Wolf

WITH AN AFTERWORD BY GERHARD WOLF

TRANSLATED BY KATY DERBYSHIRE

LONDON NEW YORK CALCUTTA

GOETHE INSTITUT

This publication has been supported by a grant from
the Goethe-Institut India

Seagull Books, 2022

Originally published in German as *Nachruf auf Lebende* by Christa Wolf
© Suhrkamp Verlag, Berlin, 2014

First published in English translation by Seagull Books, 2018
English translation © Katy Derbyshire, 2018

Published as part of the Seagull Library of German Literature, 2022

ISBN 978 1 8030 9 039 9

British Library Cataloguing-in-Publication Data
A catalogue record for this book is available from the British Library.

Typeset by Seagull Books, Calcutta, India
Printed and bound by WordsWorth India, New Delhi, India

CONTENTS

One has to blow a breath of the present into memory.

Kazimierz Brandys

1

No, that's not how it was. If you must know, the only really tiresome thing was the bickering, which didn't stop even at that point. Everyone still saw me as a child and I had stopped giving explanations, but one day I would tell them, affectionately of course because I was very fond of them; that was the thing. One day I'd tell them, I thought back then (though I never did): You have to make sure you behave appropriately. Really, that was important to me, though I don't know where I got it from—certainly not from this family. Or was it? From my mother, perhaps, whose outbursts harboured a desperate plea for dignity? Or from my father, who would deliberately ignore such an appeal because he wasn't up to it?

Oh yes, you do know things like that at fifteen. And our fathers were absent, by the way. Mine was following orders, guarding a group of captured Frenchmen—a position that was to be radically reversed later that day—marching them north-east along the very Soldiner Strasse I could see the beginning of when I looked out of the living-room window. It was starting to get light at last, which suited me fine. The morning would put an end to all the dashing and crying and sobbing. Dark rectangular blocks materialized out of the white snow; it took me a while to realize that many of the people who had passed our house during the night, or perhaps only now, minutes ago, had simply abandoned their suitcases on the path, right there on the corner. Looking out over the whole town and the river from my upstairs window, I had always regarded our house as a kind of outpost, seeing as what came after it could not be called town by any stretch. But the thought that for the passing refugees it was precisely on the boundary between hope and desperation was disturbing. For between the two lay the hair's-breadth line of indifference I feared, feared because it was a threat to me.

I was indifferent about what would happen to the gold-rimmed cups in the dining-room cabinet. Whether we should lock them in and take away the key or leave it in the door so that the enemy who would soon be living here wouldn't have to damage the furniture to get at the cups—that question left me cold. My mother rightly accused me of standing in everyone's way and not saying a word, because my real opinion would have been that we ought to march eastwards, defying our fear, head for the canons' roar to prevent, by all means necessary, the enemy from occupying our towns. At the same time, I knew, as I always did in times of disaster, that the worst they were all seeking to evade through their frantic carryings-on had already come to pass. I knew from the split-second when I woke, saw my mother outlined in the crack of the door against the bright hallway and heard her words, which were no different than usual when she woke us for the nightly air-raid alarms—Get ready, you two—I knew from the sound of her voice, which held the knowledge of the whole truth and also her horror at that knowledge, that it was the last time I would see her like that in the door to our nursery, where I had moved back in with my brother Bodo, whom I called Oddo, since my upstairs room had been given over to refugees, relatives from East Prussia. In the moment before her next sentence I had understood everything, and—perhaps because a long goodbye would have been unbearable—I had left everything behind me already, betrayed everything already, and I was horrified at myself while my mother went on: It's time. We have to leave.

You won't understand that there had never been any mention of it between us before then.

Never any talk of leaving, never of fleeing, and never of defeat. We found out only later that my mother had spoken about it, in the shop and in the inappropriate presence of the National Socialist Women's League leader, and we learnt of the consequences. The likelihood of finding out anything substantial about our parents' opinions or the progress of the war or living conditions in general was not exactly high for the children of a grocer in a medium-sized town east of the River Oder known for its well-kept parks, children who attended a high school for which their father unquestioningly paid 18 German Reichsmarks per month to the school board. Neither of us children had ever left room for doubt that we were not intending to take over the shop one day, and we were never put under pressure to do so—for reasons I understand better now than then. In any case, my brother Oddo's Christmas present was the new box for his construction set, enabling him to add an excavator to his crane system, and I went unchallenged in gathering the neighbourhood children for lessons 'on the pipes'. She wants to be a teacher, they said of me, and there was a benevolent agreement between all my teachers and all my relatives—who included accountants and master metalworkers and transport-company employees, but no teachers—and myself, a level of respect that shored me up and that I exploited blatantly whenever necessary. She came top of the class again, they'd say, or no—Only second best this year? Still. School's easy for her, she's got brains, she'll go places, you carry on being a good girl, you do work hard, here's a mark for your end-of-term report. My grandmother in Heinersdorf gave me fifty pfennigs. If you don't look after the pfennigs, she said, you're not worth the marks, when we were your age we didn't know what a coin looked like that hadn't earned ourselves.

Our Heinersdorf grandparents would be staying put, we were told, on that morning when I vowed to remember the date. It was the thirtieth of January 1945. Grandma Heinersdorf had proclaimed she'd have to be carried out of her house feet first, she'd never leave it of her own free will, and her statement matched up to our expectations. And so it was that we last saw her on our Christmas visit in the old year of '44. As always, they had lit the living-room stove for Christmas Day, Grandma Heinersdorf warming her back against it, and the crumble cake far better than anything baked these days, sadly, and Great-Grandpa was not allowed to eat with us, having no table manners and being as good as deaf anyway. Aside from which, he had his nice room and when a person is well over ninety he

does nothing but wait for death, Grandma Heinersdorf said. She was waiting for her father's death, like
my brother had waited even as a little boy for his
promised inheritance of Great-Grandpa's watch,
often teasing him by telling him to die at long last.
Great-Grandpa didn't die of his own accord at all.
Wandering half of Poland and Silesia in his youth
as an itinerant reaper gives a person strength for an
entire century. Great-Grandpa didn't want to live
'elsewhere'—he hanged himself when our Heinersdorf grandparents were evacuated in June, and
neighbours cut him down and brought the news
across the River Oder, where Grandma Heinersdorf
starved to death in a religious home that autumn.
Her grave is in Bernaux and is visited regularly,
every last Sunday before Advent by my father, her
son, and once a year by my Aunt Magda, now
known as Auntie Bremen, whom we called Auntie
Leni as children. Her name is Magdalene and she
was to leave the town along with us that morning,
this time for good, the town to which she'd had to
return ten years previously as a divorced woman
after a failed marriage to the owner of a filling sta-
tion and car-repair workshop in Schwerin—a marriage of which she will harbour grateful memories
until the end of her days. Her adopted son Achim,
whose mother was a good-looking, mentally normal domestic servant and whose father was an

SS-Sturmbannführer with no visible signs either—Achim, originally named Sieghurt and re-christened by Auntie Leni's husband, the filling-station owner, didn't do so well at school. He was proof that you never knew what adopted children have in them, but still he'd be coming with us on our trek now, at the age of ten.

Still, it was embarrassing how easy we all were to displace and drive out, compared to the steadfastness of our Heinersdorf grandparents. All it took was for the cable-radio announcer, a man usually responsible for the air-raid reports who probably egged himself on with a cry of 'keep it pithy!' every time he was about to go on air—all it took was for his voice to hold a little bit more fear, or more precisely panic, the closer the morning and the enemy inched; advancing Soviet tanks, he said, and he could have come up with no words that would have put greater fear into the hearts of the courageous population of our hometown—which was how he addressed us. I don't believe he crowed out 'run for your lives!' but I think he did manage to run for his own life after his last announcement, namely, that the *Volkssturm* militia had built barricades at the hospital on the eastern entrance to town but the district commander nevertheless advised the courageous, severely tried population of our unforgettable hometown to . . .

Those cowardly swine, said my mother. She didn't usually speak like that, or only on rare occasions, to which I will return. She didn't like curse words; she had a little more education than the wife of a grocer needs. She and her siblings, Uncle Herbert and Auntie Lissy, had attended the intermediate school on Zimmerstrasse, incidentally very close to the hospital now barricaded by the militiamen. A French teacher at the school, named Fräulein Scharnowsky and secretly called 'Mopsky' by her pupils, could not abide my mother, not for any price and not for all the years, because my mother, unaware of Mademoiselle's fear of bacteria, had started out by accidentally shaking her hand, long and hearty. Charlotte, she was told from then on, your pronunciation is not satisfactory! And even I, twenty-five years later, still suffered in my bed from the early injustice to which my mother was exposed, and gave her vehement confirmation of her impeccable French pronunciation when she sang me the only French song she knew: *Au clair de la lune* . . . She could certainly sing, my mother, no matter what that cantankerous, vindictive Mademoiselle Mopsky had to say. She had sung *Vom Himmel hoch, da komm ich her* in the church choir even as a young child, with my grandmother, a dressmaker by trade, making her a long white robe and wings stuck with gold paper so that no one thought my mother came from a poor family, even though she did. She had a bad case of tonsillitis on the day of her appearance in the cold church, but the church board pleaded that she couldn't let them all down and sent a closed coach with two horses to collect my eight-year-old mother with her angel's wings and my grandmother, who was now locking all the doors upstairs in her flat, and take them to the Concordia Church. She sang like an angel, they said, and then took to her bed for three weeks.

It was different for the East Prussians and the West Prussians than for us. I had been watching them for weeks since school no longer took place, or rather became a place for the refugees who bedded down on straw in the classrooms and especially in the gym. It seemed to me that these people were, for some reason, better cut out for the trek than we were, having developed practical techniques in their everyday lives and a facial expression that I simply couldn't imagine in us. And as we grew up in times when the phrase 'to each his own' was very much on the air, I had no doubt that taking flight was not for us. The more familiar the names of the places the refugees told us when we handed them herbal tea and bread and mettwurst, the denser and hastier the treks whose participants now responded with nothing but scornful laughter to our suggestion to take a rest at our home, the more stubbornly we refused to speak about it. To be sure, cases were packed and bedcovers stuffed, secretly, by night presumably, as it now emerged. I was not let in on that secret, as usual in such cases, because children must be spared, children need not know everything, children must have a happy childhood despite all that happens, children blab unintentionally. Or intentionally.

Children know nothing.

I reacted to this suppressed knowledge with floods of tears, which my mother called a fainting fit—She's overstrained herself, the poor child!—and had our maid Elli cure with a big cup of hot peppermint tea. You stay at home tomorrow, dear, don't you go to the refugee care group, I'll call your teacher. She did just that and so it was her, my mother, who last spoke to my beloved teacher, Fräulein Dr Strauch, who displayed her fullest understanding and accommodation and expressly praised my devoted work. But my mother still didn't want to take in the little boy, not even until his mother had given birth in peace, an imminent event, as the midwife had assured her in my presence in the overcrowded Hermann Göring School gym. Not, however, until she had managed to warm up her feet, there's nothing doing with cold feet, young lady, not one baby in all the world goes to a mother who has cold feet. No, said my mother, we can't take the boy, what are we to do with him when we . . . She would almost have said it out loud had I not immediately burst into my fit of tears, related not only to the missing half of her sentence that I did not want to hear but also to the small, stiff package I had removed from one of the refugee waggons that evening and passed on to my mother, who unwrapped it and broke out in screams. Temperatures of twenty degrees below freezing were not unusual that January and it was impossible to indefinitely keep the temperature in a trek waggon up to a beneficial level for a newborn baby, as everyone realized, but I didn't want to see the frozen child, I wanted to rid myself of the stiffness remaining in my arms, I wanted to do a good deed and take the pregnant woman's little boy home with me, I wanted to believe I could still offer my home to other people without deceiving them —but I couldn't manage any of it, and so I burst into tears and drank the hot sweet peppermint tea in large gulps.

It embittered me that the Führer's portrait was being torn from the walls in all the houses in town.

Our Führer was an oil painting, sixty by forty cen-
timetres, dressed in tones of grey. A red ribbon ran
around his elegantly tilted grey peaked cap, the cord
at the front also grey. He didn't look at us, instead
gazing rather precisely at the sliding glass door
between the dining and living rooms, a door that
made my friends consider our home modern, and
displaying his strong, straight nose to us in profile
along with a single grey-blue eye, which was rigid
and which we therefore thought was firm. He gazed
firmly. Not always, Fräulein Dr Strauch had told us
when we talked about the uprising of the Goths—
'Who weep for brave Alaric, the best of their men
lost'—not always are the traits of the Germanic race
clearly visible in our fellow Germans, although that
would of course be desirable and was being fos-
tered. The Führer in any case, who was at least
dark-haired, she said, and apparently also dark-eyed
(the painter of our grey-blue Führer's eye had probably succumbed to the desirable racial traits)—the
Führer united the decisive innermost Nordic traits,
she told us, to wit: courage, rigour, constancy, willingness to fight to the death and German thought.
I knew that the doubt in our return to this house,
to the desk with the accounts books at which our
father sat every Sunday morning, with the pale
space on the wall where the Führer had once hung,

was doubt in the Führer. For that very reason, I despised those now tearing his picture from the wall, smashing the glass in the yard by the bin and stuffing the canvas and the wooden frame in the heating furnace. My mother did not neglect to demand my diary from me and burn it along with the picture. It would serve them right if I joined Operation Werwolf, but who was to tell me where it was?

Even the shop had been packed up, as it turned out. For the last time, my mother removed the safety bar from the door, without which the insurance company would have ignored any break-in, something that had never happened, and unlocked the door after carefully drawing the blackout curtains, and my grandfather rolled out the butter barrel while I carried the pail of strawberry jam. The butter went rancid over the spring but the strawberry jam lasted. For a long time, rancid butter with strawberry jam was foisted upon us as the best of all possible dishes, but now the butter in the barrel was still fresh, and outside, as mentioned, it was twenty degrees below freezing. Do I have to tell you everything, my mother complained, and we took off our coats and tugged a second sweater over the first. Things you wear on your body, my grandmother said, are hard to take away. They all had their experiences of flight, they had all lain awake at night and wondered whether to put on two sweaters or possibly a cardigan over one of the sweaters, and had decided on the two sweaters. Above my grandparents' wooden beds hung a chubby-cheeked embroidered angel in a black frame, resting his chin on his hand and pondering the embroidered motto: If even hope's last ship departs, do not lose heart. Now that it would have been necessary, they couldn't follow those instructions. It was clear enough that the 'East Prussians' were sitting on packed cases—Auntie Anni with her darkening hair roots and her now-fallow energy with which she had run an entire carriage company in Königsberg, the 'dollies', her twins by the names of Gina and Gitta who were of different heights and weights, and her son Dieter, the same age as Oddo, whose innocent, nay sensible expression concealed uninterrupted adventurous undertakings, in which my brother embroiled himself unthinkingly so that even I could not obliterate all traces of their almost criminal activities. Incidentally, I was not told for a long time that it was the two of them who had singed undeveloped films in the toilets of Hermann Göring School (which we both attended since the girls' high school had been turned into a military hospital); but I guessed at enough of their nonsense that I felt a tremor when an extensive investigation was begun into a case of defiling the flag. It was not them who raised the sack on the flagpole, but they did know the perpetrator—a weak, pale boy from their class, Hanns Fischer, a mummy's boy driven to an act of desperation by envy of his classmates' gang activities. No one gave him away, incidentally.

It was time to say goodbye. The gesture with which my mother threw her silver fox back in the wardrobe for good pained me more than the thought of any loss of my own. That gesture was perfectly fitting for the situation; at last an occasion had arisen upon which she could construct larger gestures. It was her exploitation of minor occasions for major scenes that had driven me to my reticence. The girl's got so quiet, no one has a clue what she's thinking. Without a moment's thought, I could have answered a recent survey by the teacher I adored above all else, Fräulein Dr Strauch, about the 'worst feeling', by writing down the word 'shame', but I was ashamed to do so and wrote 'fear'. That is a surprise, said Fräulein Dr Strauch, I wouldn't have thought that of you. I remembered that a German girl knows no fear, but what should I have written? Perhaps a German girl knows no bad feelings at all. My friend Hanna had written 'disappointment' and Dora, who had only come to our quiet town a few months previously—as our headmaster had said at the flag ceremony: in the course of the implemented evacuation—from bombed-out Berlin, Dora wrote 'envy'. All of them better than fear; what devil had taken hold of me?

Now I could have told my teacher—who incidentally stayed in the town and died shortly later on a transport headed east, arrested as a high-ranking Nazi functionary—now I could have told her that a mixture of all these bad feelings is probably the worst of all. Yet I said nothing and nobody knew what I was thinking, as usual.

Not for a moment did I think of saying goodbye in front of everybody else. There was no point in treating me like a child, there was no point in making that instruction public, now of all times, now that every second was valuable, there was no point in recommending I take a last look around, because I wanted nothing other than to forget these desolate, degraded rooms as soon as possible. Which I managed entirely, so that nothing remains to me of that morning but my mother's outline in the door, my thumb on the knot of tightly packed bedcovers that had to be tied together, the Führer's portrait, the empty space above the desk, the gesture with the silver fox, at which I had so often blown against the growth of the fine, downy fur when my mother laid it around her shoulders over her coat, making it bristle in waves, and that minute in the hallway, opposite the telephone whose number I shall never forget, no matter how quickly I lose track of every other number: 2592. Who was I to call? I picked up the receiver—the line was dead. I no longer recall whether the door to the hallway or the front door was open, as I think I remember because an icy draught came about, although that was not necessarily from outside. Something occurred, I can't explain any more precisely than that. Perhaps you'll understand what I mean if I say that the appearance of the stone guest in *Don Juan* unerringly reminds me of that moment on that morning to this day. Terror, Fräulein Dr Strauch. Terror is the worst feeling. Have you never felt the tiny hairs on your back stand on end?

The girl has flights of fancy, and then again she lacks imagination. Now, for instance, she's standing there by the telephone, she's lifted the receiver for a moment and put it down again with great caution, and as usual no one knows what she's thinking, but she's thinking that she can't imagine how anyone is supposed to return to a house abandoned like this. For they're all only preparing themselves for days, perhaps weeks, until the Führer and Supreme

Commander will have launched the reserves at this section of the front. They're not taking any summer clothes, they'd laugh at the very thought, and this child, who does believe strongly and without doubt in the Führer, suddenly no longer believes in a return to this, her parental home, and she says not a word about it. She knows, or she wishes without admitting it, of course, that she may one day be capable of thinking of this moment correctly—that is: justly. For injustice is perhaps the very worst of all the worst feelings. She doesn't know that some types of justice take years to come about, decades in fact. Then there'll be a photo of this very parental home, which she really has never seen again, as though she had a promise to keep. That photo shows her white two-storey house gnawed by the tooth of time—there was no fighting that far out of the town. It shows the rock garden on the right of the entrance run to seed and the little poplar on the corner as a tall tree. It shows, on the slope on the left where sweet clover used to grow for the rabbits, a wonderful bush reaching up to the bay window of the dining room, and that must be the little acacia cutting. It shows that the sign painted by my father announcing 'Electric Mangle' has been removed as expected, likewise the bicycle stand outside the shop and the red wooden letters that ran around the double-windowed shopfront on a projection from the outside wall: Grocery, it said on the Soldiner Strasse side, Delicatessen and the name of the owner, Uhlmann, on the August-Wilhelm-Heinrich-Strasse side, the street on which we lived, as one of two houses. The second was the architect Frithjoff's 'Haus Leonore', half of which has fallen victim to a fire, however, as the photo reveals. The sand hill has been dug away, a blunt cone with a diameter of at least two hundred metres consisting of nothing but the very finest gravel and pure sand, no playground could be more ideal, and we would never have expected it could be removed. Why not, though; it was previously high and probably peaked and overgrown with knotweed and gorse, known then as Gallows Hill, and my grandfather witnessed the last hanging there in his youth. It was a murderer, he told us, but sadly I have lost track of the precise details, which my grandfather retained faithfully in his memory until his dying day. In any case, however, they wanted to name our short road 'On Gallows Hill'— an imposition for a grocer's shop, a choice behind which my mother suspected malevolence, spurring my father in vain to take a sharp tone in his letter to the municipal authorities. My father did not take a sharp tone in correspondence with authorities, but my mother did wrest the phrase 'disruptive to enterprise' out of him, albeit inserted into a polite sentence. The administration granted our complaint and our short road was given the name of a prematurely deceased councillor of unknown achievements—They did that on purpose, said my mother. My father had forced the authorities to make a correction and he showed me the paper with the town seal on it as I stood beside him at the desk in the new room with the silvery shining wallpaper, the new Führer hanging on the wall, the sun shining in, and my father a determined man who could be relied upon. I was seven years old and we lived for three more years in the new house until the war began.

So they have removed the sand hill in the photo and built terraced houses, probably using large-block construction, probably for the Polish employees in a number of factories that have also been newly built. Yet I am still standing in the hallway, in that icy draught coming from outside or some other place, refusing to walk though the rooms, wondering whether my grandmother has remembered to take along the picture of my mother as a young girl that she had on her wall, a beautiful young woman with a gentle face, dark sparkling eyes and a large hat. I was very fond of that picture,

I loved it, if that word is permitted, but not so much that I'd have asked after it. My grandmother hadn't taken it with her, my grandmother had taken all the keys to all cupboards and doors, for people surely weren't so bad that they would break open doors, and after her death in Lutherstadt Wittenberg they found all the keys in a little pouch in among her paltry linens.

Nor did we lug along the thick brown photo album that lived beneath the shelf of collector's cups in the dining-room cabinet and had taken on its very peculiar scent. Of course, such a photo album would be the first thing I'd reach for next time, although my regret at its loss has proved to be more superfluous the more time has passed, for I can effortlessly conjure up all the family photos, although I can't show you them but only describe them over and over. It may be that it bores you already, the naked three-year-old girl with the page-boy haircut, a garland of oak leaves draped diagonally between her legs and across her small body and a crown of oak leaves set upon her head, instructed to wave a bouquet of oak leaves. I did so. You were such a lovely child.

So my feeling did not deceive me, that I could do without everything, that there was nothing for me to insist upon. For I could still look at the picture of my mother as a young girl later on, as often as I wanted and even until tears came to my eyes, if I needed them, and I could hear my grandmother's voice along with it. I still can if I want to. Your mother was such a young thing back then, that was when she'd just started at Ardolf's, at the cheese factory, she was a bookkeeper there, senior bookkeeper even, your mother was a hard worker and old Mr Ardolf let her bring cheese home for us, that was a great help after the war, you wouldn't credit it! You had to be always on the ball there, my mother would say when she was with us, and I can still hear her if I want to. Then they put me in charge of all sales to Berlin and I went over every fourteen days, I had my regular room in a good hotel, in the middle of the inflation, you wouldn't credit what it was like! But no one tried it on with me, believe you me.

I believed her, still believe her, always will believe her and I'm passing it on to you—my mother was a hard worker, and she was beautiful, and no one tried it on with her in her youth, because it always depends how well a girl is brought up and how she behaves. She was brought up strictly and righteously, and she behaved well, and I was expected and wanted to do the same and so I would never admit to myself that a violent expulsion from thoroughly familiar circumstances inevitably means a transfer to thoroughly unfamiliar circumstances, about which one might over time—not right away, but at some point—become a little curious. I would have despised myself, had I pronounced inside myself in exact words that the bright wallpaper with its bouquets of blossoms in the nursery, which had seemed to me a particularly congenial miracle on the first morning when I awoke in the room, had grown rather pale; to be precise—although I was not so precise to myself— a little dull. Did the children to whom I had read Sleeping Beauty or King Thrushbeard only the day before yesterday, perched on a box in the gym of the Hermann Göring School, leave behind the same kind of wallpaper? Had they also, as I of course did, left their fairy-tale books at home? It's a shame about the book, I might have pinned onto the wall the glossy picture page on which I had scratched the wicked queen's eyes out with a needle. I had also scratched out the red, poisoned half of the apple, incidentally, creating the basis for the endless stories that we, my brother Oddo and I, told every night, to produce a thoroughly happy version of Snow White assured against any form of danger. We never doubted that we were brother and sister for that was the foundation of our world, but in low voices, tightly wrapped in our bedcovers, we some-times raised the tension by asking ourselves whether our parents might not really be our step-parents? And were perhaps very good at pretending? And pulled faces behind our backs that hailed misery and disaster? We may never have caught them pulling faces, no matter how often we turned around as quick as a flash, but did that really tell us anything? A shudder of blissful horror when our mother appeared in the door—her outline!—and admonished us sharply to go to sleep. The certainty that she was not our stepmother, however she might scold, but merely hated us getting too little sleep. And so in urgent cases we were to knock on the wall and obtain the other's permission to speak. Oddo knocked and I bade him speak. He demanded short and accurate information on how babies are made. I was flattered but not sure I could accept responsibility for telling him. He however, dutifully knocking on the wall and awaiting my permission for every new sentence, invoked his dangerously poor memory, which guaranteed he would have, by the next morning, forgotten everything, *everything*, I tell you! of whatever I revealed. It mattered to me that Oddo, nearly four years my junior, found out in a decent way, unlike me, though I have not borne any lasting harm from the cold-blooded explana-tion by a neighbourhood child. So I knocked on the wall, he gave me permission to speak and I told him. He was silent for a second, knocked on the wall, received permission to speak and announced that he had thought something along those lines and it was rather a shame that he'd have forgotten every last scrap of it by morning. Then we were both quiet for a long time, leaving our various thoughts in peace to think what they liked, but just as I was about to fall asleep Oddo knocked again. Go on, I whispered, but keep it short! Oddo asked merely: Us too? At which point our mother shouted from the hall, asking whether we really wanted to drive her to absolute desperation. I whispered without knocking: Go to sleep! What do you think? Us too!

I wouldn't have wanted to go without that but I didn't have to go without it because I took it along with me, and what use was a last look at the nursery? I knew there was no snake between our beds, although it had writhed about there night after night for a long time, as thick as a tree trunk and vicious as a murderer, making it impossible for me to leave my warm soft safe white bed in the darkness. The floor was taboo—I was not allowed to touch it with the tip of my toe, on pain of death. The girl's very nervous, she's overstrained, she reads too much, now she's started calling for us at night, what next? But the snake didn't come from my books at all, it came from one of Grandpa Schnauzer's two stories. To distinguish him from Grandpa Heinersdorf, he was called after the little dog, a miniature longhaired terrier, with whom I shared my first games and who shared his bone with me, walled in under the table by the grownups' legs. The snake came from the story of the woodcutter boy who sat down on a tree trunk after a long day's work in the forest and ate his sandwich, until the tree trunk beneath him started moving and out of the previous year's dried leaves came a burrowing snake as thick as a tree. The boy apparently got away with a shock and his hair turned white, but the snake stayed on the floor by my bed, especially since, in the gully we weren't supposed to walk through at dusk because of the vagrants who were said to have lingered there in the old days, by broad harmless daylight a man with black curls and a grim face had drawn a long snake out of his trousers in front of me. An event I by no means understood but did not mention out of caution, because it had gone into my flesh and blood that everything unfamiliar automatically gave grounds for concern. Thus, we made no mention of the smashed cup, which was of course discovered in the bin and led to a slap round the ear, in front of all the other children to boot; we made no mention of my brother Oddo's membership of the Soldiner Strasse gang, for which I was useful because I could spot the approach of the Lehmannstrasse gang from the attic window and signal in good time; we made no mention of our nausea after our first attempt to smoke cherry leaves in tobacco pipes; and we even made no mention of a case of tonsillitis, until my brother gave it away with his lump-throated speech. I didn't like to lie, only doing so in emergencies, which I shall come to later, and every lie I told shocked me and stayed with me a long time. But I was an expert at the technique of pious hypocrisy and non-mentioning, and it weighed on my conscience, which was trapped between my concerned mother's strict rules and the necessity of everyday life as a fifteen-year-old. And so on that morning I went as far as the megalomaniacal thought, short but intrusive as a bolt of lightning, that this entire great expulsion might be nothing but a pretence, to liberate me from my compulsion for exaggerated testimonies of attachment and sympathy, beneath which, I knew in my heavy heart, grew a terrible indifference that no one could forgive, least of all myself, although I did know how much I felt sympathy with others. Leading me into a state in which it did not seem absolutely impossible, at least, that entire armies of tanks might be set in motion to redeem me from my entanglements of full and semi-dishonesties.

Don't forget what a wonderful childhood you both had! My mother had words like these at her disposal, she would put her hand on your shoulder to say them, and there was no face you could present to words like that. Why are you acting so stiff? We did have a wonderful childhood and now it's over, we were walk-ons in a play guaranteed a happy ending on the days of our birth, and now they were casting us into the midst of a tragedy, its laws absolutely unknown to us—although it is a little flattering in the far corner of one's conscious mind to be entrusted with such a difficult and productive role. Fear immediately ceases once the loss one trembled at the thought of has come to pass. All at once, the thin dew of boredom that settles on circumstances too long immobile is blown away.

You know how large and complicated my family is. Today they are scattered, and you don't even know all the members; at that time the family was concentrated in our town through birth, a tendency for solidarity and settlement, through greater than average cohesion and various blows of fate—divorce, bankruptcy—that enforced return. And to my admiration and unease, the family had carefully prepared their joint withdrawal from the now-unsafe town like a family excursion to nearby Altensorge. The lorry and trailer that stopped outside our door belonged to Hannemann and Son, Wood and Coal in Bulk, Transport Company, to which my Uncle Alfons had preserved a loyal bond through thick and thin since his apprentice days. A bond, incidentally, that the family noted not without disdain. Uncle Alfons works like a navvy for that Hannemann, and what does he get out of it? He's exploited, that's what he is, he begs for more, he dances to Hannemann's tune, unconditionally. No, that was not what the other men in the family wanted, to be a boss' doormat, but who was it now bringing the lorry to save us all? Not my father, mangling his school French with the prisoners and headed north-east to the point, only hours away from him now, at which those fear-inspiring Soviet tanks, approaching from the north, would cross Soldiner Chaussee, only to hurry on to the more southerly Küstriner Chaussee, which was thus open for us for a few hours longer; my father was out of the equation, for a long time. Not my Uncle Herbert, my mother's brother, our favourite uncle because he had a sober and just mind, because he had made it from a simple metalworker to a foreman at the Mischke and Co. agricultural-machinery factory, where he ended up producing some kind of artillery components, however, and was deferred from the war but also from our escape. He had sat his wife Aunt Lucie and my cousin Gabi down on the back of the lorry, waved goodbye and headed off to work with his tattered briefcase. The former husband of my Auntie Magda, who had already taken a seat with her adopted son Achim on the trailer, was out of the question because he was far off in Schwerin, and anyway divorced. And Auntie Wilma's husband Richard, from whom she wasn't divorced, was a subject to be avoided entirely. And so we were left with Alfons, Alfons Schawein, whom no one had taken seriously even as a chief clerk for the company. He came along with the lorry, he gathered us all up, he sat behind the wheel and issued instructions, he pushed back his cap, wiped the sweat off his brow and urged haste. We had to look him gratefully in the eyes that were slightly too close together, we had to tell Auntie Alice, his wife whom we children called Lissy, how capable her husband was, and we had to realize that this finally emerging capability on Uncle Alfons' part made that terrible day a little better for my Auntie Alice.

I shall provide proof later on, but for the moment you must simply believe me that sixteen members of our family, represented by the main surnames Uhlmann and Janowsky and by the branches Schawein, Bieder, Bunge and Feinlich, were seated in Hannemann's lorry when Uncle Alfons gave the command to depart and clambered behind the steering wheel in the driver's cab. His breath steamed out of the side window as I was still outside, could still turn my head to the four Bahrsch Buildings consisting of six two-to-three-room flats each, which had played a role in my father's calculations of anticipated custom and in the third of which, ground floor on the left, lived the Hitler Youth junior leader Horst Binder, who followed me all the way to my accordion lesson with a demonic look on his face, prompting me to falter even more in my resolution to practice the Danube Waltz and *Es zog ein Bauer ins Heu*; Horst Binder, who was to use a weapon of unknown origin on the evening of that same day to shoot first his parents and them himself, at the age of sixteen, not wanting to fall into enemy hands or fearing perhaps more than anything else the discovery that twenty-four hours are still a day and a night, even once the enemy had captured his and soon everyone's hometown. I was able to walk over to the right of our escape vehicle and look over to 'Haus Daheim', where the two daughters Lore und Eve took the same walk to school as me but had never quite been my friends, not even when inviting me to birthday parties in their house, set far back from the street and made inaccessible by high fences, inside of which everything was perfectly normal, if a little old-fashioned. I could see the entrance to the 'gully', a small chain of end moraines into which a valley—the gully—had been scored and trampled into a path, where all our toboggan runs were, the bumpy run and the devil's run and the giant run, where I had broken off the tip of my ski. Then I could look back again, down Soldiner Strasse, along our house—the living-room window where I had sat and read *Miss Sara Sampson*, nursery window, bedroom window, outside staircase, rock garden. Then Frithjoff's house, far in the background the blocks of flats on Fennerstrasse, all our customers, in the foreground the clay pipes that had been waiting for years for underground cable work once planned and then deferred due to important war projects, the sand hill, behind it and above it on its own hill the Strantz barracks, field kitchen full of pea-and-ham soup on visitors' days. And that's it.

I don't know now who pulled me into the lorry, all I know is that my mother pushed me from behind, and that I then held out my hand in turn to pull her up, that she grabbed my hand and put one foot on the edge of the trailer, gave herself the impetus to climb up and then suddenly collapsed back, letting go of my hand.

No, said my mother. I can't. I can't go with you. I have to stay here.

Another feeling, Fräulein Dr Strauch, another one I could have added to the list: incredulous horror.

2

My mother was not in accord with the life she had to live. The picture of her in her youth that I knew was not in accord with the mother I knew; that was why I loved the picture, but also why I hid that love like something forbidden, with the sharpened sense of the inappropriate that children develop in families that deceive themselves. Sometimes, on my grandmother's birthday, my mother would sit at the extended table right underneath her picture, and then I'd sit down opposite her and compare her to herself. The result was different every time but I didn't know what caused the greater or lesser similarity to her photo. All I know is that I laughed when she was cheerful, and that I felt safe from all perils when she was in the mood to mock my habit of removing the crumbly top of the cake and eating it last of all, instead of forbidding me to do so as she sometimes did. My brother Bodo and I were giddy with delight when she sang *Am Brunnen vor dem Tore* and *Ein Wandersmann mit dem Stab in der*

Hand, kehrt wieder heim aus dem fremden Land. Auntie
Lissy could try all she liked, she simply didn't have
our mother's voice or her love of music, though she
usually asked my father in vain to switch off the
Hamburg Harbour Concert or the Wehrmacht
Request Concert and treat her to the *Kleine Nacht-*
musik, as my father held the view that no one could
possibly enjoy it, and anyone who claimed to do so
was pretending. *Sah ein Knab ein Röslein stehn*, my
mother sang, but sometimes she wouldn't even
come to the birthday celebrations. You go down and
have a word with her, Herbert, she listens to you
more than the rest of us, and what's the matter with
her anyway, sitting down there like that and crying?
What do I know, said my father; so he didn't know.
Charlotte was having one of her turns again, she
was making mountains out of molehills again, she
was taking everything far too seriously again, we
can say what we like after all, you can't go weighing
up every word, where would it end? Spoiling our
birthday party like this; and goodness me, think of
the children!

My father's knowledge of how to slurp an oys-
ter out of its shell and how to get used to such a
tasteless and slimy but nutritious dish was down to
his stay as a prisoner in Marseille, where the locals
at first called them 'boches' and threw stones at

them when they were driven though the streets, which just went to show how full of hatred the French were. Oddly enough, this knowledge, his two attempts to escape from imprisonment, punished by detention without food or water, the fact that he had 'lain at Verdun' at the age of eighteen, hearing the angels sing in the skies—none of that weighed as heavily as the pound of capability that my mother, who not yet met my father, had obtained at home in the meantime, as senior bookkeeper at the Ardolf cheese factory. Everyone conceded that my father had first had to enjoy life a little after finally being liberated from his years of imprisonment, only my mother made an impenetrable face on the subject. But all that was before my time, before the birthday party of one of her workmates, Mieze Riekmann, a funny young bird, pretty false by the way, and quite a looker, you could say, but unmarried. Old Mr Ardolf had to let her go later on, she was making eyes at his son young Mr Ardolf, and that's understating the matter. But anyway there was plenty to drink at her birthday parties and my father was sat to the left of my mother as her dinner partner. Mieze Riekmann and my father had a friend in common from the rowing crew, Gustel Scholz, he was a great fellow, always good for an adventure and we had plenty of them, us lads from the rowing crew were the talk of the town back then. So was your father, said my mother, proud all of a sudden. He was a bon vivant, and his clothes—always tip top! But of course he had a drink too many, and I wanted to sneak off home but I hadn't reckoned with your father. I'll see my dinner partner home, oh yes I will! he called out, always the man about town, your father, always a man of the world, and he did walk me home, just don't ask how! We laughed until we cried, how funny our mother was, how much fun it had been to start with for our parents, what a nice person that Mieze Riekmann was, never mind all her scheming and plotting, and what a looker, who cares if she was making eyes at young Mr Ardolf— was there any crime that wasn't more than recompensed by inviting both Fräulein Charlotte Janowsky and Herr Bruno Uhlmann to that significant birthday celebration? Oh yes, said my father, beer and various spirits and not much to line my stomach, I couldn't really take it. My mother set him down on the stone balustrade of her front garden, on Küstriner Strasse, I know the house, I know the balustrade. My mother slipped like a flash in the front door, ran up the stairs like a flash, crept quietly but still like a flash to her room and looked out of the window. And to this day no one knows how that man, drunk as a skunk as he was—our father, we laughed ourselves silly—how he got down from that balustrade. And do you know where I spent that night? We knew it, we choresed it every time, but we wanted to hear it over and over again—in the municipal park! Twenty yards away from the duck pond, drunks have their own guardian angel, and a park-keeper shook him awake in the morning and issued the unexcelled statement: I thought you were a corpse, sir! I thought . . . We nearly suffocated. A corpse, sir! Twenty yards further on and you two would never have . . . That's chance for you, first Verdun, then the dangerous work on the overhead power lines at Marseille, and then the duck pond in our local park, always in our favour, as it should be, a good person never goes under. But the next morning he called me up and he said to me: Do you know, Fräulein Charlotte, where I spent the night last night? No, said my mother, your grandmother I mean, that drunk young fellow?

Nevertheless, Bruno Uhlmann stopped enjoying life a little on the day of his marriage to Fräulein Janowsky, he put it behind him and no one had ever tried it on with her anyway, she was twenty-six now and he was twenty-eight, and they set up their first grocery in the Fröhlich Building on the corner of Küstriner Strasse, living in a single room behind the shop and a dark kitchen, and when I was born three years later in that hard winter in the middle of the depression, the stories of which have survived, the milk froze in my bottle and my father's customers had more debts than money. That's how we started out and it wasn't exactly a piece of cake, and sometimes we had to clench our teeth, believe you me.

In the picture with the big hat, my mother looked as though the photo had been taken before the teeth clenching, and perhaps it had. I don't know when the face I knew settled over that early face of hers. I'm trying to pick up the threads of her life and I can't find the turning point, can't find the end of her youthful face. One thing is odd. During their engagement they went to Dievenow, treated themselves to a trip to the Baltic that was much talked about as an unprecedented luxury. They brought back a photo, in shades of brown, I remember, that was also in the thick brown photo album. They had stood in such a way that you could see all the luxurious advantages of the trip at once—the sea, the beach and their woven beach shelter. I can see them clearly, my grandmother in a flowery dress with an expression of pride and satisfaction that she simply couldn't supress, my father at the end of his enjoying-life period in the suit my mother often described to us, complete with straw boater, pale jacket and cane, and a pince-nez perched on his slightly surprised face. But try as I might, I can't see my mother, who was of course in the photo. I have a feeling she was sitting in the beach shelter, in a white dress—yes, I'm almost sure of it. But was her hair cut short by then? Was she laughing? Or am I borrowing her expression from that other picture where she's holding me in front of her, only a few days old? Her hair is cut short there, she's laughing there.

Perhaps she didn't yet hate the shop back then. She was a lover of rigorous words and she knew how to use them. She'd say, how I hate this shop, I can't tell a soul how much I hate it! In the middle of the war, in the middle of that time of greatest silence—a silence I did not feel within me until much later, but then as a lack, as a flaw indeed that could not be put right—on an autumn evening at ten past seven, ten minutes past closing time, in other words, my mother took the big key ring with all the shop- and cash-register keys on it and threw it at the feet of the constable who found our shop open ten minutes too long and wanted to fault it as unfair competition. She threw the keys at him, I can still hear them clanging on the terrazzo tiles, and she shouted that he should go ahead and lock her up then, go right ahead, then at least there'd be an end to all her hard graft, then at least she'd get a lie in, then he could stand behind the counter and calm down the women, him or one of his bigwigs up there. The grey-haired constable beat a wordless retreat, tiptoeing backwards while my mother was not finished by a long shot and was digging a hole for herself with all her talking, as my father sometimes predicted. With all your talking you'll end up digging a hole for yourself, my girl! I've had it up to here, my mother shouted after the constable, indicating the level with one hand, above her mouth at any rate. I hate this bloody shop, she yelled after him, one of those occasions for one of those expressions she otherwise avoided.

Come now, do calm down Frau Uhlmann, said Frau Blankenstein, the wife of Blankenstein the lawyer, for whose sake the shop was still open because she always came in just before closing time so that my mother could slip her a piece of margarine or an eighth of raisins she sometimes squirrelled away for good customers. She came when the shop was empty because she sometimes had to exchange a word or two with someone about her husband's professional experiences, which he barely mentioned to her. My mother would send me upstairs, saying she didn't need me any more and I should take the telephone up with me and the box of coupons, she'd be right up. She sent me to the same Frau Blankenstein on the night when she had the terrible stomach cramps. Run over and ring the bell until she opens up, tell her I need a doctor, she'll know what's the matter. Stiff with fear, I lay in my bed afterwards and heard Frau Blankenstein talking on our telephone. Yes, it's urgent, she said, yes, immediately, the poor woman's bleeding to death. I leapt up and ran to my parents' bedroom. My mother said, you go and lie down, it's not for you to see, don't be scared, it's not bad. But your father knew all about it and still went to his EDEKA night, she said as she was on the stretcher, as the men carried her out past me. He knew all about it and he still went. When he came home, after midnight, he smelt of alcohol and I felt sorry for him because he was so shocked. I began to suspect he had gone out so as not to see his wife being carried away. I told him she'd been bleeding, I gestured at where, I didn't know a word I could use but he understood me and he was grateful while not explaining anything. Aunt Lucie, the wife of our mother's brother Herbert, came the next morning to stand in for her at the shop. My mother was over the worst of it, so I heard, and perhaps it was better that way, Aunt Lucie said, what would Charlotte do with a third child, what with her work and in the middle of the war?

I don't know when I began to sense my parents' gloomy secret: that my mother hated the work we all had to live from—although she never failed to be an extremely competent businesswoman—and that she silently accused my father of having dragged her into it. She grieved for all her lost possibilities, but because it wasn't her way to suffer in silence she found a hundred pretexts to convert her great disappointment into myriads of minor complaints, in a constant gruelling battle against going to rack and ruin—the spectre that haunted her the most—and in her permanent concern for us, leaving us only our retreat to myriads of minor misdemeanours. Is it true that you were up reading until one in the morning? Don't you fib, a customer saw the light on, you'll ruin your health. Don't read so much, you'll spoil your eyes. Go outside instead, you need fresh air. And the early morning scenes when there was once again no evading a new gruelling day for her, when the maid came five minutes late, when one of us hadn't yet packed our school bag, when I couldn't find a glove. You'll go to rack and ruin, can't you see I can't take care of you all the time! This is how it starts, my God, whatever did I do to deserve this? I haven't forgotten the deep breath with which I closed the door behind me. Once, she'd been watching me from the shop door and she called after me: You go up and clean your shoes, you don't go to school with dirty shoes, once and for all. Where would it all end!

And she was never there. Oh, for a chance to stroll around town with my mother like any other child, to go to Café Kraeger for éclairs! Do you want to so much? Well, we will then. I'll take a couple of hours off and we'll go to Café Kraeger! We sat at a little round marble table and the staff knew my mother—Really, you've got such a big daughter? There were some kind of potted palms and it smelt like paradise. I had the best mother in the world. Oh child! she said and laughed. You've still got your work crown on, we'd say when she stayed at the table for a minute after lunch, and we blew at the short hair pressed to her forehead. Oh children, you're so silly. We'd play mothers and fathers, Bodo the father, me as the mother, and my dolls Lieselotte, Hertha and Pudge were the children. Hertha was my favourite doll; she had belonged to my mother and she had real hair. I thought it was my mother's hair and I'd sniff at it. I knocked Pudge so clumsily off the cupboard where she lay in her bed that her head slammed against the wall and broke in two. I set up a heartrending hue and cry, thinking such pain would never be healed, and my mother came dashing in fearfully but found her worst fears were not confirmed. She took the broken doll carefully in her apron, said that poor Pudge was very ill but it wasn't incurable and she'd take her to the doll's hospital, everything would be fine. Now I knew what bliss was and I wailed with joy. My mother suggested we christen the new dolls' tea set. She made semolina with us on the dolls' stove, the new dolls' plates had a gold rim that dissolved good and proper in the semolina, and all three of us laughed terribly at the golden semolina. I've never tasted anything like it, I said.

Or I threaded beads for my mother and the cotton thread broke when the necklace was all but finished. And it was going to be for you! I sobbed, so she gave me thick yarn and wore the necklace I made her all evening, and she looked beautiful. And then again she couldn't get over the fact that I'd put the potatoes in the saucepan unwashed. Clumsy, oh how clumsy! she said over and over, until I rebelled and asked her if she'd never done anything wrong as a child. No, she said, not such easy things, we had to work much harder.

There was the argument between her and our father over whose family had been poorer. Only a quarter pound of sausage a week, said my mother, and my father got that on Sundays, we'd get a swipe across our bread, and then my mother kept a goat, but don't you go thinking the milk was for us, she sold that and all. And chickens in the first place, and then she took in sewing. My mother only ever worked. She barely mentioned her father, Grandpa Schnauzer, but I didn't notice that. He'd been laid off in early retirement. There was a shortage of work at the Reichsbahn and a surplus of ticket clippers, that's how it was in those days. Oh, you don't know the half of it . . .

Our father was hurt at being told he didn't know the half of it, because if anyone knew poverty then him, and more than once he walked us past the basement flat on Schönhofstrasse to show us where he'd lived as a child. Do you think anyone would have even listened if I'd told them back then I'd have my own house one day? You could have been a teacher, Bruno, said my mother, and it pained me to think that my father had been offered another life than the only one I could imagine. He came to visit us specially, my teacher Herr Meyer, your son's been top of the class for years, he told your grandfather, I can apply for a stipend for him, let him be a teacher. And what did your grandfather say to that? It was one of the stories with its own breathtaking internal drama that I loved to hear over and over. Well, you know what he said, you know him well enough. Nonsense, he said, the boy's going to learn a proper trade and nothing fancy like that. And he sent me to old Mr Fröhlich for my apprenticeship, maybe that was a good thing too. A starveling schoolmaster? your grandfather said. Don't make me laugh!

You shouldn't have chickened out, said my mother, you should have got your way, and I shouldn't have got myself locked up in that cheese factory, what were the Ardolfs to me anyway? Mind you, old Mr Ardolf always treated me decently . . . I should have done my midwife training like I always wanted to, then things would be different now. And anyway . . .

They'd forgotten us. I listened with unease as they invented different lives for themselves. Yes, but then they'd never have met? Yes, but what about us, our appearance doubtlessly prepared well ahead by a chain of set coincidences? On the other hand, I was upset that my father no longer had the slightest prospect of making a teacher or a doctor out of himself and perhaps being admired by his wife for it.

And yet she must once have admired him, or at least she did admire him in my very earliest memory. There's a warm brightness around us, we're sitting at a round table, my eyes almost on a level with the tabletop, and opposite is my father, of whom I see nothing but thick, frozen-red fingers in gloves with the ends cut off, fingers starting to glow and tingle in the warmth and being rubbed and stroked by my mother. I've never managed to find out why the fingers of his gloves were missing, but I do know now that the scene took place during the winter when my parents ran two shops for a brief while, the one in the Fröhlich Building on Küstriner Strasse, in the allegedly meagre back room of which that warm lamp hung, and the new shop on Sonnenplatz, the corner shop in the new Gewoba Buildings that no one had wanted to take over in the midst of the crisis. But my father, 'a grocer through and through', spent a long time pacing the neighbourhood with pencil and paper, looking at the shops already there—badly run tobacconists, that much was clear—and calculating how many people lived in the Gewoba Buildings, considering methods for wangling custom away from Rambow's Grocery down on Friedrichstrasse, and he took out a loan and ventured a try. And then he cycled all the way through Friedrichstadt to Sonnenplatz every morning. He wrote on a blackboard that the first customer got a bar of chocolate and the fiftieth too, and at four o'clock that afternoon he called our mother to say he'd just given away the third bar of chocolate and his day's intake was higher than the Küstriner Strasse cashbox on a Saturday. Would you believe it, said my mother, I went weak at the knees, I had to have a sit down, and then I ran across the road and left your great-grandfather alone in the shop for a moment—there's a picture showing our great-grandfather next to the shop door in the Fröhlich Building, a blue apron tied around his waist, holding the handlebars of the delivery bicycle, the company name legible: Grocery Delicatessen Bruno Uhlmann—and then I said to your grandmother: Mother, we've made it! And then she made a good pot of coffee, and you, Helene, were playing in your corner with Schnauzer, and I picked you up and told you over and over: We've made it, Helene, we've made it!

We knew when to take a risk, said my father—who dares wins.

3

No one wanted to believe her but I knew my mother well, often predicting her words and gestures; I can still feel them in me now with the compulsion to repeat them. I knew she would stay there once she'd said it. I knew my grandmother was trying in vain, calling out: Charlotte! Think about what you're doing! Think of the children! I knew my mother would entrust me with my brother, who was only twelve, as she then really did; I knew she would promise to catch up with us quickly as soon as it got dangerous, telling us not to be afraid, she wouldn't come to any harm; I knew she would assure us she'd find us wherever we or she ended up; I knew we were to meet up in any case, if we missed each other, at our Uncle Wilhelm's house in Kirchmöser near Brandenburg, number 12 Seestrasse.

Only Charlotte could think of a thing like that, everyone said as my Uncle Alfons angrily slammed the cab door and angrily drove off. He couldn't stand the woman and that was nothing new. Everyone talked about my mother and stared at us but we didn't cry. I said loudly, She knows what she's doing, and then they fell silent. I saw my mother in the slim gap between two tarpaulins that formed the rear wall of the lorry, saw her getting smaller and smaller and then I couldn't see her any more but I still saw the house, and then the angle was too sharp to see and the sand hill pushed its way in front of our house. I heard someone speak the indignant word 'orphans' at the back of the lorry, and I took my brother's hand and was surprised to find I wasn't upset but merely dulled in my senses. I thought that my mother had never showed herself more clearly than at the moment of her leaving us. I was very close to the secret she had always hidden from us, and my desire for my mother's secret vied with the hurt that she'd abandoned me for . . . For what, in fact? And what was she doing all alone now?

She went back to the abandoned kitchen and made coffee, tidied the rooms a little. Then she set out for the Strantz barracks that we could see from our house, and made her way stubbornly all the way to the local commander, whose wife was one of our customers and received deliveries once a week from the apprentice Erwin on the delivery bicycle. The officer's horror that she had not yet left town, the panicked leaving activity in the barracks, the hopeless expressions on the faces of the hurriedly retreating soldiers, either very young or aged—all of this convinced her more than the trembling radio voice of the town's impending doom and of her right to abandon her post. She ran to the factory where her brother oversaw the production of some kind of arms components. They'd received no evacuation order. She managed to convince her brother he was risking his life for nothing and that the enemy was at close quarters. She made lunch for herself and him, opened up long-hoarded tin cans. Eat, Herbert, make the most of it, who knows when we'll next get a decent meal. She packed a briefcase for him and a shopping bag for herself, full of food and cigarettes. She asked him whether to lock up at all and did in the end, but didn't look around again. They took the gully to Küstriner Strasse and walked the road we had driven twelve hours previously, in among exhausted late-leavers. On their left, the last train westwards passed them on the tracks. Imagine we'd tried to catch it! The train was held up and the tanks approaching from the south shot it into flames, by which point my mother and my Uncle Herbert were sitting in a post-office car taking the last sacks of mail across the

River Oder, the driver having accepted cigarettes as their fare. The twelve-hour delay, however, had made precisely the difference between flight and chaos, between the enemy approaching and the enemy at hand. Don't ask me what we saw, she told us later. On the west bank of the Oder, the bridges were being prepared for demolition and hastily drummed-up war-weary men on leave formed special Wehrmacht units. Anyone who saw what we saw, they'll know victory is up the spout, my mother said, and she asked everyone after us. Nobody had seen the lorries with the name Hannemann on them.

By then, neighbours had broken into our house and taken away what they could make use of. My mother had heard the shots from the eastern edge of town and it's true, approaching shots override the laws people have previously obeyed. The picture everyone has stared at as if hypnotized has a longitudinal axis; it rotates and its terrible, wild reverse side becomes visible.

Why was Sonnenplatz not enough for my parents? When did they begin to regard it as a stopgap? Sonnenplatz? my mother would often say later. That was just a stopgap. All at once the table was covered in floor plans as soon as the plates were cleared away, neat drawings. The architect is very capable, it was said, he knows his business, but of course we have to keep an eye on him. We're building, you see, and in an area everyone has warned us against. But we'll soon prove them wrong. We'll see what we can get out of the place when we set about it the right way. Grandpa Heinersdorf said: Don't overestimate yourself, my boy, but Grandpa Heinersdorf had been saving for a house for years, putting aside the pennies from his railwayman's pension—he had made it to an engine stoker—and the gratuities from the sports association where he worked as a groundsman. We now knew where to go on Sundays: to our building site. We now always had a destination, the two of us crawling around in the unplastered innards of our house, me walking my new route to school and inspecting the neighbourhood for other children. We also knew what we were saving for. You know we have to save, we were all agreed because the most wonderful new life was about to begin, in the most wonderful new house. We didn't ask as children where the money came from; words like 'loan' and 'mortgage' were uncharted territory for us. I was allowed to attend the topping-out ceremony; my brother already had the measles, which I got straight afterwards, but I was healthy for the topping-out ceremony and sat next to the bricklayers on planks laid across trestles, and fished for sausages in the big pan and knocked my lemonade bottle against their beer bottles and toasted the house builder with them, who was mighty generous with the bottles, but that was my father; he knew how to treat people. My mother said so that evening, and the next morning she put me to bed and drew the curtains because measles patients aren't supposed to have light, and our doctor came, long tall Dr Schröder, whose daughter Gundel I'd have given anything to have as a friend, but she kept to chubby little Uschi from her neighbourhood. Well, well, said Dr Schröder, now at least we both had sweet little polka dots, praise and glory be to him upstairs, that's a promise, and the lady and gent can keep each other entertained.

As I was very big, though, almost seven years old, and my brother only three and a half, I was in charge of providing entertainment all on my own, and at the end of our weeks as invalids every inch of our room was covered in a tiny miniature town, the inhabitants all created by us and provided with names, their lives put at our disposal. We were the absolute rulers of our town, we took note of every insubordination that occurred and took strict measures. Herr Müller from number 25 hadn't turned up for work? The miniature police came to pick him up. Ingeborg didn't want to do her homework? Ingeborg was locked in a dark room for three days. Served her right. Above all, we punished every attempt to deceive us and conceal any violation of the laws. Strangely, being expelled from our town was the severest penalty for all its inhabitants. We were about to move into our own house, where everything would be precisely as perfect and beautiful as in our town, the existence of which we kept as the highest and ultimate secret between us. It was impossible to conceive what would happen if one of us broke that secret. We made our most impenetrable faces when our parents trod carelessly on our houses, not knowing a thing about them, and I made my brother swear—on pain of hell, death and the devil—that we would never betray our town until our dying days.

And then, when I woke for the first time in the new house and couldn't get my bearings because the wall on the other side of the bed was different to usual, an indescribably bright sun shining straight onto the flowered wallpaper we had picked out of the big book of wallpaper samples, I thought that now our whole new life really was beginning and I might never encounter greater fortune and happiness.

I don't know what my mother thought on that morning, when she woke up in her bedroom with its brown pearwood furniture, alongside my father in their marital bed. But I do know what face she wore as she went downstairs to open the shop door together with my father, although it might not have been necessary for her to go with him because there probably wouldn't be such a crowd on the first day that more than one person was needed. But she wanted to see the first customer, she wanted to shake her hand personally and introduce herself, and she wanted to weigh out little bags of sweets for the children, handing them over with her best regards to their parents. I would never have thought a grocery shop could be run like a conquest, like an expedition to unknown, possibly hostile terrain, but precisely that was the view that satisfied my mother's ambition. Incidentally, she only wanted to conquer because they really were the best, because no other grocer served his customers as fairly, because the women got recipes and tips on childcare from her along with their impeccable goods, because she never fobbed anything off on the children sent to do the shopping, and because she was no more polite to the major's wife than to the wife of the street sweeper—or only polite in a different way. The very idea! You mustn't

let casual customers know they're casual customers; that's the only way to win them over as regular customers. But then, you have to give good
customers the feeling they're part of the family. By
all means, Herr Uhlmann, your wife is the soul of
the shop! My father acknowledged it, saying: If I
didn't have you, my girl! He was still saying it once
his wife had long since begun to get bored of all the
heavy work again. It turned out that sugar and flour
were weighed out and handed over the counter in
the same way everywhere, that the chat and gossip
remained the same in all the town's shops, that it
was easy to predict the monthly intake fairly precisely after a while, that they'd never have any trouble paying off the mortgage on the house but
they'd never be able to live like kings. My father, a
man who liked to compensate, got elected onto
the EDEKA board, the Purchasing Cooperative of
German Grocers, and went to its meetings and
social functions. My mother said she had no desire
to be swung around the room to awful music by
some fat man who reeked of alcohol. You always
have to be so harsh! said my father and went on his
own. Mother let me sleep in his bed and waited for
him. He came home as it was getting light outside,
stood swaying in the bedroom doorway and complained in slurred words at being booted out. Me,
your husband, Charlotte, you won't let me in the

bedroom! You vagabond, said my mother, you vagabond!

Vagabond, she called my father a vagabond, I thought to myself, feeling that each of them was both right and wrong, and not knowing why they were incapable of seeing and respecting the other's point. I didn't know why it was so hard for anyone to do right by my mother—for all our maids, most of whom were patient and hardworking but in my mother's view tended to let everything go to rack and ruin if she didn't keep a close eye on them; for my grandparents, who now lived on the top floor of our house and tended the garden as best they could, not an easy task with the sandy soil in our region, who had to make sure the swastika flag (One's enough, my mother said) hung from the crown of the roof on all high days and holidays, and who appeared punctually on the first of the month with their rent book and paid their 32-mark-rent; and for us too, who also had a tendency to be lax in matters of order, to let things go to rack and ruin, and that was what my mother simply could not put up with, once and for all. She came to the conviction that it was she alone who kept the new house and the whole family from going under, that the entire burden of everything, whatever that might be, lay on her shoulders and that no one was prepared to acknowledge the permanent sacrifices she was forced to make. We all fell under a permanent feeling of guilt towards her; it shocked her when she noticed it but she could do nothing to change it. It was true after all—they needn't have built the house if everything were to stay the same afterwards, but nobody could have compelled my mother to admit to her great disappointment with life, and so she worked like a woman possessed on the image she had created of herself and of us: an exemplary businesswoman, who then really did run the shop alone after her husband was drafted into the Wehrmacht, whose children were exemplary students and extremely talented, whose domestic conditions were in perfect order in every respect, and whose house was tip-top. I saw with anguish how she needed help and demanded help but was incapable of really accepting it, because everyone had their own way of helping her, not her way. I saw that a person can or perhaps must hate the thing they live on and I saw that work is a burden. I loved my mother and was loved by her and remained always in her debt. I secretly took the key to the stockroom next to my bedroom on the top floor and helped myself every evening to a bar of flaky chocolate out of a box that grew alarmingly empty. I lay in bed, sucked on the chocolate and read, and despite my guilty conscience and despite my fear of discovery I was happy in a seclusion that lasted perhaps a matter of hours. I got into the habit of distancing myself from the tensions, which I could neither fully understand nor ever reduce. I wrote, suddenly gripped by fear of transience, of the terrible emptiness from which my mother had suffered for years, in a secret diary that my mother demanded from me on the day of our leaving—so she did know about it—and burnt in front of me.

I felt that she was right, in her way, with her decision not to leave 'all this' in the lurch, while not really understanding her, as the shock that she was leaving us alone in a dangerous situation with no real necessity came too unexpectedly and thoroughly questioned all security attached to her up to that point. Later, when the distance to the events made it possible to judge them justly, I understood that she couldn't let pass this opportunity to prove something to herself. She stayed behind and proved to herself that her life had not been a failure, that the house and the life she'd led in it were worthy of protection, at the cost of sacrifices, the greatest sacrifice conceivable—by wagering her children. She proved that this home was not a pile of bricks she had to leave behind, nothing unbearably banal, as she herself had oftentimes thought, but the meaning of her life, her idea of duty and work and living together, which was not to be abandoned at the very first signal. She proved a sense of duty, more than was necessary, loyalty, more than was demanded, she proved independence from the family's judgement, which had formed in the departing lorry in the very same second as she said: I can't go with you. I have to stay here.

4

None of us guessed that we were on an arduous but beneficial journey. Only with reluctance, great reluctance did we face the possibility of important experiences. It's easy to say, after the fact, that we wouldn't go without such experiences, but while a person is bumping along the cobbled roads she knows best of all the roads in the world, and while she is already noticing the sack she is sitting on pressing uncomfortably because some hard objects have been roughly packed into it, she wouldn't of course have the idea of considering herself lucky to be travelling for at least fourteen days in this cold—that was impossible. We would just cross the River Oder, the Oder being a barrier that no enemy could ever cross, and we would wait there until our Wehrmacht had restored the normal order of the world.

The day was grey. I saw next to nothing through my gap between the tarpaulins and the trailer behind us. I heard motion on the streets, carts, cars, shouts, but I saw none of it. I saw a tiny section of the road driving past, the houses at about the level of the first floors, sometimes the tips of a fence if it was tall enough, tree trunks close below the leaves, bushes. But it seems as though I had seen everything precisely, and I still see it now.

I see the Yellow Peril moving past, a conglomerate of dirty yellow two-storey workers' housing, inside the buildings worn wooden staircases, small front gardens with low green picket fences and the large, trampled square of grass where callow boys would stand around in groups with their bicycles on summer evenings, sometimes noisy but sometimes so quiet that I was overcome with a terrible yearning whenever I walked past at a distance. Other than that, I knew little about the Yellow Peril; the working-class children went to the lower secondary school, rarely appearing at the Young Girls' League, and there was no point, people said, in insisting they attended regularly. In the 1920s, people said, the police had not dared set foot inside the Yellow Peril, and the reds had hidden their fugitives there. I connected the name Yellow Peril with those wild times, the days when cudgel-swinging communist hordes had sought to prevent the Führer and his followers from taking the only correct path for Germany. The men who disappeared behind the doors of the Yellow Peril at five every evening, though, had no link in my mind to the earlier cudgel-bearers, and if anyone had asked me where the latter had vanished to, I would surely have been most amazed and at a loss for an answer. But of course no one ever did ask.

I knew more than saw that after the Yellow Peril on the left-hand side came the square covered in trampled knotweed that we crossed every morning to shorten our route to school—at least as long as I still went to the girls' school—but that twice a year, at Whitsun and in October, was crowded with carousels and stalls and changed overnight into a fairground, where it was possible, unlike in the big bare space, to get truly lost. A tune came instantly to my ears and I was instantly sitting in a car on the caterpillar ride with my friend Hella, who was allowed to celebrate her birthday with us at the fair, something none of us would have begged out of our mothers, but she did. We rode endlessly until I began to feel sick but I was afraid to get off. Everything's spinning, we shouted and yelled; Hella had brought along a small bottle of liqueur which we all sipped at during the ride. The carousel's gramophone blasted out *Auf dem Dach der Welt, da steht ein Storchennest*, the same tune over and over, and by the third time we were singing along. On the roof of the world, there's a stork's great big nest, with a sweet little babe for me and you! A couple of young soldiers on home leave, in the car behind us, offered to come to our aid, bawling out: If you'll be my girl then I'll wear my wedding vest, so you can get a lovely baby too. I saw myself sitting in the car, heard myself giggling as I didn't usually giggle because I rejected such vulgar behaviour. I was interested in whether I wanted to accommodate the soldiers, how much longer I would hold out on the ride as I felt worse and worse, I was interested in what I'd say if one of them, the black-haired one, were to speak to me, and then the ride stopped, our money was all gone, I felt sick to death and I had not the slightest desire for the black-haired soldier, who went off incidentally with a curly-headed girl in a red jacket. Malicious, unrestrained envy assailed me, binding that whole afternoon up with the ride and the old song and the black-haired soldier so that I kept it in memory, for without that envy, directed at nothing particular, certainly not at the very ordinary soldier with the very ordinary girl, I'd have forgotten it all immediately.

In fact, it is only feelings that anchor our experiences in memory, and only if the worst of all maladies, emotional coldness, has befallen a person do life's minor and major experiences slip through them as if through nothingness, and the only torment that remains is the torment that they can no longer torment themselves about anything, not even that. But on that morning I was not cold but numb in my feelings, like going deaf after a grenade hits close by. Everything I saw and heard sank to the bottom, and only much later could I fetch it back up, awaken it to life and summon the appropriate feelings. So I often recalled the Adlergarten, the place on the opposite side of the street to the fairground, a pub for the workers from the Yellow Peril but with a built-on functions hall in which our elementary school celebrated its large school festivals in the early years, where I once—at the age of nine, I think—had to sing a night watchman's song, in a costume I was proud of and that must have made me look absolutely ridiculous, with a halberd stuck with silver paper, produced with great care by my grandfather on his kitchen table with the aid of a whole battery of the sharpest cobbler's knives.

> Hear ye, hear ye, gentlemen,
> Our night bell has just struck ten,
> Ten commandments from on high
> That our Lord you shall obey.

I held the lantern clumsily in my left hand and the light tipped over and went out, and behind me the choir of fellow night watchmen sang:

A watchman's eye is not enough,
The Lord God must watch over us.
So thank Him, who on this night
Guards our lives with all His might.

The song had ten verses and the contrast between the cold behind the stage and the warm hall made my nose run, meaning I had to wipe it on grandfather's jacket sleeves, but the audience thought that was part of my night-watchman's manners, rewarding me with rousing applause and nourishing my unfortunate love of stage appearances and recitations, for which I soon began writing my own texts and learning them with my classmates. We expended particular zeal on a spring play, in which I appeared as a snowdrop in a short white voile dress, from beneath which peeked a pair of brown woollen tights knitted by my grandmother, on which my mother had insisted so that I wouldn't overcool my innards. That was a kind of idiom in our family, in which the spectre of incurable abdominal diseases made an early appearance, diseases that could lead to absolute childlessness, as we could tell from Auntie Magda and Auntie Wilma, my father's sisters. Their lack of children had other causes, however, which I only learnt later, although Auntie Magda—whom I called Leni because her name was Magdalene and she was very fond of pet names—

although she would have told me everything without hesitation, being a very trusting soul. Yet like everyone in the family, she had terrible respect for my mother, which my mother accepted as absolutely deserved because none of all these women, some of whom didn't know how to do a decent day's work, some of whom didn't even manage to hang onto their husbands, could possibly hold a candle to her.

It's true that none of them could be as fundamentally desperate, without regard for those around her, as my mother; it's true that she intimidated us with the boundlessness of her desperation and that she left us behind at such moments without so much as looking around. Like on that morning—still in the Adlergarten but in another year, August 1939, and this time not in the functions hall but in the courtyard, where the white garden tables with the green crossed iron rods supporting them had been crowded into a corner to make room for the men who had to report there at ten o'clock on the dot, depositing their tied-up Persil cartons along the fence and then standing together in groups or perching on the garden chairs and offering each other cigarettes. It was a hot day but there was no beer on offer, no band playing like on other Sunday afternoons, and I occasionally stuck my little finger in my ear and shook it to shake out the water that dampened all the sounds. But there was no water in my ear; the voices were dampened of their own accord. The women who had accompanied their husbands—like my mother with my father—spoke quietly to them, the men spoke quietly to one another, as if embarrassed—an embarrassment I couldn't explain, but which weighed down on me because I always found it hard to bear adults' embarrassment, and when one of the children made a loud noise everyone called the child to order. The men asked each other when it was going to start at last and I wished too that it would soon start, despite not knowing what, for I had never seen men enlisting. Stop your worrying, the men murmured at their wives. Is there a war on? No. As long as there's no war on, no one's going to get shot for goodness' sake, and if all goes well I'll be back home the Sunday after next because the whole thing's just for practice, of course, we do have to be prepared for emergencies, so it's silly of you to look so down in the dumps. Only the commands cut loudly into the murmuring and brought it to a standstill, only the commands swept the men into their places in rank and file and the cartons away from the fence, and all at once the courtyard was so empty that twice as many people would have fitted into it. All at once I trembled and wished it wouldn't soon start, but then came the command and they were already moving off, all of them at once, out of step; the soldiers who marched past our house to their parade grounds from the Strantz barracks were much snappier. The men were even more embarrassed than before, waving with arms half-raised, each wishing his wife wouldn't cry, but all at once they all broke out in loud sobs, even my mother, and they all walked alongside the column, us too. A song! came the command, and, at the peak of their embarrassment, our fathers began to mutter: *Muß i denn, muß i denn zum Städtele hinaus* . . . Go back, Charlotte, said my father, who was marching on the outside close to the pavement, to my mother, and she obeyed him without contradiction, something she never otherwise did. So we went back, my mother crying loudly all the way from the Adlergarten to our house, up the road we had just driven down in two minutes in the Hannemann lorry, holding her handkerchief in front of her eyes, wearing her white shop coat and crying, and my grandfather, Grandpa Heinersdorf, laid his hand on my shoulder so heavily I can still feel its pressure today, and said: You won't see your father again, my girl! I said not a word, as always, unable to cry, unable to speak and crushed by a dull sorrow and by the feeling that something forbidden was happening. Except I couldn't have said who had forbidden it and why the Führer, who guided everything for the good of us all, nonetheless insisted on it.

A little way below the Adlergarten, a lane joins Soldiner Strasse at an acute angle, known as Schlachthofgasse or Slaughterhouse Lane, a sloping road onto which we now slid more than drove in a large, careful arc on the iced-over surface. I only caught a whoosh as we drove by of the narrow cobbled alley between the houses, leading directly down onto Küstriner Strasse towards the entrance to the Germania Cinema, which showed the second-rate and old films and where the usherettes didn't pay such close attention to our age as in the Kyffhäuser Playhouse, so that we, forever not-yet-sixteen, went there to seek albeit delayed knowledge of the movies that simply had to be seen. *Der große König*, for instance, starring Otto Gebühr. I really was almost the last girl in class to see it, apart from eggheads like Editha, who was at least as swotty as she was ugly and who belted out the song *Santa Lucia* in our music lesson, a name that stuck. My mother, however, proclaimed that all the great kings and all the Santa Lucias in the world could go pot-roast themselves for all she cared, and refused to give me permission for the cinema, reducing me to spending an entire overcast afternoon gazing out at the town through a veil of tears from my pitying grandmother's window, cultivating a dark sorrow within me.

Then we were passing the Fröhlich Building on the left-hand side, at the same time as Slaughterhouse Lane turned onto Küstriner Strasse, with the old shop we had left behind us so long ago, and on the right-hand side the Schnauzer grandparents' old house, where the Ardolfs' cheese factory was still running in the courtyard, mainly producing low-fat Harz cheese just like after the First World War—a house my grandparents had moved into from their railwaymen's flat thanks to old Mr Ardolf's intervention, and from which they later moved to Adolf Hitler Strasse, which old folks still called Heinersdorfer Strasse, where a wonderful yellow poplar grew in their otherwise narrow and meagre front garden, and from where we then had them move into our new house, on the top floor where two rooms and a kitchen had been fitted out to their requirements, not with central heating like in our downstairs apartment but with stoves, because my grandmother wanted to sit on her seat against the stove to warm her back while she read the *Landsberger General-Anzeiger*.

Now we followed the tram tracks straight through all of Friedrichstadt, past Fischerkietz where the southern exit to the 'gully' was, in a world unfamiliar to me while its entrance, only five hundred metres away, was my closest home territory. Had I only stuck my head through the gap in the tarpaulin—but I didn't—I'd have seen once again the four railwaymen's buildings, undecorated like two-storey barracks, in the second of which my mother had grown up with her brother Herbert and her sister Alice, by the light of a smoking petroleum lamp that always played a major role in my mother's memories, although I was not to find out why until later on.

That was my first route to school, from Sonnenplatz to the Pestalozzi School, sometimes walking and sometimes by tram, and then I'd sit next to Christa Huth from my class, a weak, pale and sallow-blonde girl, whom my mother suspected of having consumption, telling me not to get too close to her. I told her so one day when I grew tired of her constant declarations of friendship, at which her mother appeared at our front door to complain and I denied even mentioning consumption, but I tugged my mother into the corner of the nursery and whispered to her, Yes, I did do it, you said so yourself! But I said it to you, silly, my mother whispered back,

not for you to go telling her! And she went to the
front door and told Frau Huth the whole thing was
a misunderstanding, no one thought her daughter
had consumption, and told her to take her a bar of
chocolate to calm the child down. For a few days, I
walked all the way to school or skipped a tram,
and then we soon moved house and Christa Huth
wasn't in my class any more. We heard she was sick,
something to do with her lungs. You see, said my
mother, I can't understand mothers like that who
don't notice anything's wrong with their child.
That's the least you can ask, and I only hope you
didn't catch anything from her. When I did catch
something from a classmate just as my mother had
always feared, years later but not far from that
January day in 1945 I am still writing about here,
my mother couldn't warn me beforehand because
she didn't know the girl at all and she wouldn't have
been able to tell she was sick. Yet always, over all
the years, she expected the worst every time we left
the house, and every time we were late home she
would take up her post outside the shop door or
telephone the whole world, and she was only satisfied once she had us all 'under one roof'—which
hadn't prevented her from sending us off all alone
on the most dangerous expedition anyone could
have thought up for us, compared to which a simple

cycling tour or scouting game or swimming trip were not worth a mention.

My aunts and my grandmother said all this by turns in our lorry, and I thought that way at least they might forget they were driving through their town for the last time. They so easily forgot what had just troubled them; the only thing they never forgot was humiliations, which they dragged after them all their lives, as if attached by an indestructible thread. For me, however, it once again struck me as clear as a blow that this was the last drive, an irrevocable journey, as a nondescript dirty grey house slid past my viewing slit. I knew the house; it was the front part of the building where Snow White lived in the back—an old woman with tangled black hair and a muddled head, emaciated down to the bones, with skeleton arms that were the first thing to jerk out of her kitchen window when we, our satchels on our backs and fired on by older children, had sneaked round the back to her flat and called out 'Snow White, Snow White!' After her arms came a stream of curses, which we had to answer with loud laughter—that was the rule. And then came—hoped for and feared with galloping hearts—Snow White herself, sometimes with her grandchildren in tow, dumb limping Hannes and Edith, who may have been of sound mind but also stuck her finger in her mouth because everyone expected it of her. Snow White scolded and ranted, but we scattered in ecstatic horror, regrouping at a safe distance and calling out: Snow White! Snow White! Where are the seven dwarves?

Where was Snow White now, though? Where was dumb Hannes and where Edith, whose grandmother had always twisted her hair into a 'roll' and fixed it on her head with grips—Edith, who wore dresses that were far too large and had to fold the sleeves of her jackets twice over?

Nobody saw me crying. I put my face close to the gap, an icy draught drying my tears instantly and not a motion to betray me to the people behind me in the lorry, my family who would probably stare at my back and exchange pitying looks at my slightest twitch. I didn't twitch.

5

If it's true that a person who prepares, in the midst of difficult or unexpected painful events, to tell their story later has an advantage over their fellows and perhaps fellow sufferers, then my advantage began on that journey. I already knew that my feeling of having to remember everything precisely because someone might one day be interested in it was rather foolish; everyone who might be interested in such fates had been dragged into them themselves and had no need for reports on the hideous events they were experiencing at first hand. Despite that, I was compelled to memorize everything, putting me at an ever-greater distance to my fellow travellers, whose only wish was to forget the present and cling to the rose-tinted past. At the very moment when I had begun to suspect that this war and the genuine misfortunes that occurred in other people's lives and in books were not meant for me, a suspicion that grew into almost disappointing certainty, someone had wanted to teach me otherwise, that much was clear. Now, that someone was watching me to see whether I showed signs of learning, but I had my beautiful, unjaded pride, which I could gather up against that someone, feeling ready for hand-to-hand battle. I was pessimistic for all the others in our truck, though, who were still silent as if numbed but whose moaning and groaning was bound to thaw out soon enough and then be impossible to silence.

Another thing I could have predicted was that my Auntie Magda would be the first. She could never keep what she considered her feelings to herself for more than five minutes. I was convinced that was what had ruined her marriage to the filling-station and car-repair-workshop owner in Schwerin, not the vile intervention of his redheaded secretary, although she was presented to us as cunning and depraved enough—albeit in the absence of our parents, who would have strictly forbidden my unfortunate Auntie Magda from making such comments. And so it was she who could stand it no longer, who put her hand on my arm—she always had to touch everyone she talked to—and said in a muted voice that we were now passing the place where we had once been so happy with our dear parents. She spoke about our parents as though they were dead, and by 'the place' she meant Sonnenplatz. I also disliked her abuse of the word 'happy', but her whole life was founded on that abuse.

Here, at the end of the No. 5 tram line, was where my mother had waited with me in terrible impatience for the tram to arrive at last, to depart at last and take us to the doctor, who was expecting us so that he could remove the bead I had stuck up my nose, precisely one day after my mother's dire warning. I had rarely seen her so aghast and disappointed; she couldn't stop asking me whether she hadn't told me, just yesterday, how dangerous it was to stick a bead up my nose, and did I not believe her, could I not obey her, did I now at least see what I got out of being so stupid. The bead was propelled out of my nose with a stream of blood, the red flowing onto the doctor's white rubber apron. What a disgusting mess, said my mother, and all because you can't do as you're told. It wouldn't have taken much more for her to apologize to the doctor on my behalf. I'm going to have to take away all your beads, she said on the way home. Go on, then, I said, I'll get new ones. I was five years old and my mother didn't reply, out of surprise I assume, and she left me my beads in the end.

I really don't know why I have kept that unimportant story of the bead in my memory so precisely and have much more trouble remembering that other, much more significant story that also happened right there at the last tram stop. It was the time when we almost saw the Führer in real life, the only opportunity ever offered to us, and it went without saying that we, my mother and I, walked down the three hundred metres to the road where other people had been standing, most of them women, for hours as they said, since dawn, since the news of the Führer's intention to visit our by no means significant town had gone around like wild-fire—that was what they said, wildfire, and I saw the fire running wild. It was the first time I stood among excited people, regretting not clutching a bouquet like some other children, amazed at the courage of two girls wearing white dresses and garlands in their hair, who stretched a white ribbon across the road to bring the Führer's car to a stop and tell the Führer, right there on the edge of our town, how happy he was making us all with his visit. I have the feeling a lot of women wore their hair curled at that time and I vaguely remember, small as I was, seeing those curly heads against a remarkably blue sky, and I feel as though an ebb and flow of murmuring sur-rounded me, seeming both sweet and scary, making me both excited and anxious. My mother, incapable of doing nothing even then, deployed persuasion and frenzied activity to push us children into the front row. There we stood and waited for the shining car that would bring in its wake a blessing for us all, worthy and unworthy, and a curly-headed woman behind me told her neighbour how jealous her sister in Pomerania would be when she wrote and told her she'd seen the Führer, whom they could obviously never expect all the way out in Pomerania. Who knows, said the neighbour, you never know with him. You're right about that, said the curly-haired woman, but you've no idea what a tiny out-of-the-way hamlet my sister lives in!

A loudspeaker car came along and told us which towns and villages the Führer had passed through on his triumphant trip to the Neumark and about the 'indescribable' welcome he'd been given there. It was clear to me that 'indescribable' meant there were no words to describe the welcome, and along with the loudspeaker man I feared that we, who had to give the very first impression of our town, might fail, that our enthusiasm would wane compared to the other towns, that our welcome might even be describable. I had to concede to the loudspeaker man, who found it inconceivable for our reception not also to be 'overwhelming'. He encouraged us to rehearse, and suddenly a wave of screams broke out around me that I couldn't explain straight away. I thought he was coming now, the Führer, and when I realized that all the curly-haired women and their children were screaming for the loudspeaker man, as though they had built up great horror or great desire inside themselves that they had to shout out at any price, for whomever's sake happened to come along, I was ashamed because I had witnessed a transformation of everyday people. It was the same shame that took hold of me when Hansel and Gretel's parents, who were thought good and caring, cruelly took them into the forest to starve. I never wanted to hear that part, didn't want to imagine the parents' late-night conversation and their hypocritical smiles the next morning. I wanted to know nothing of the wilderness that grew inside all people every night, for that was how I imagined it—a jungle inside every person, shooting up insanely every night, every morning newly broken, worn down, trampled. Friendliness and smiles by day, primeval jungle by night—it was all in the fairy tales. And now that the loudspeaker man allowed them to, the people were screaming out their jungle call in broad daylight, with carefully set curls, bouquets in hand, at the No. 5 tram stop, which was of course not in use that day. Just like the non-running trams—I thought now, and it frightened me—everything could be suspended by the curly-haired women's screams of joy, everything we usually held by, the alarm clock ringing at seven in the morning, school starting at eight on the dot and meals at the allotted times, to which the curly-haired women, as I knew very well from my observations in our shop, submitted themselves with cast-iron precision. I felt as though they were screaming like that not out of joy but in rage, but the loudspeaker man praised them very highly and drove on into town, to rehearse the welcome scream all along the route.

I don't know whether we stood there for much longer or only briefly before the second loudspeaker car came along and announced in a monotonous voice that the Führer had to break off his journey prematurely because our fellow Germans had held him up too long in their enthusiasm. We were to go home. I thought it impossible and inappropriate to go home without having used the real scream I'd heard rehearsed, but the crowd didn't clamour loudly for their scream, merely scattering with disappointed, sobered murmurs, and the shame I expected did not come about.

I wish I knew—but do I 'wish'?—why I stood amid the crowd and waited trembling for a glimpse of the Führer. What did I imagine: the man from the weekly newsreel, standing in a car, staring straight ahead, his arm stretched out at a right-angle to his body? But I hadn't yet seen any weekly newsreels. Who had taught me to wait for him? I wish I could say, but I don't know.

What I do know—or think I remember—is this. My childhood bedroom on Sonnenplatz, my bed protruding into the room, differently to the way it stood in my later, 'real' memories, the blue-striped curtains drawn; it is early morning I think (although this is very unlikely), in any case, grainy light. My parents are both standing by my bed, my father wearing a strange dark peaked cap and a yellow shirt, my mother seeming cheerful. She says: Now your father's a member too. Her relief carried over to me, but not until much later could I explain the incident to myself. My father, incapable of making a decision of his own accord, had been forcibly incorporated along with the entire rowing crew into the *Marinesturm*, a waterborne sub-organization of the SA. He couldn't refuse, he believed, and he didn't have to fill out an application form. The relief I remember so well was the relief of the little people who had been granted a brief respite before the millstones ground them up between them.

I have no more explanation for why I stood by the side of the road, aged five or six, and waited feverishly for a Führer I must have been told about, who must certainly have been spoken of in glowing tones in the shop, where I sometimes lingered to open and shut the flour and sugar drawers when my father had bags to fill. Or had they let me listen to the radio, a black box made by Telefunken, to the reports on rallies in which the speakers almost burst into tears of passion? From times of which my memory has fewer gaps, I know that my mother tried—usually in vain—to keep me away from such presentations, allegedly because they got me too excited; in reality, though, because they made her uneasy, because she feared my willingness for devotion and an instinct warned her against allowing me too much enthusiasm. It was all too easy to become 'spoilt', a word that made a deep impression on me along with the conviction that children are easily spoilt goods, rather like bananas for instance, which my father had to sell below price if they took on black bruises. But these goods in particular offered a chance for profit and a risk for a good grocer; no business could flourish, of course, on sugar and flour and semolina and groats, which stood around in their sacks in the shop's back room for for ever and a day, never changing their price and never spoiling. But tropical fruits and the first tomatoes and the equally easily spoilt kinds of sausage— they were the signs of whether a grocer knew his customers and how to deal with them. From such conversations at the dinner table, I constructed the insoluble link between easily spoilt goods and easily spoilt children, and I was terribly shocked when I found bruises all over my body after a fall, for the signs of my spoilt nature were now becoming visible for all, just like with bananas.

How strange. I have the feeling that this is the point, to understand my five-year-old's enthusiasm for the Führer, where I ought to relate a tiny insignificant incident that occurred later, when we were living in the new house and I was probably eight years old. My first, effusively adored teacher, Herr Warsinsky, had asked the class, presumably while instructing us on hygiene, who did not wash in cold water in the morning. Along with a few others, I had raised my hand. What? Herr Warsinsky said to me. I'd never have thought that of you! My mother was very angry. She got me to feel the water that ran out of our bathroom geyser in the morning. Was that what I called hot? Lukewarm at most, and I could truthfully have called it cold. What must Herr Warsinsky think of us now!

That was the beginning, as far as I know, of the chain of scenes between my mother and me concerning the highest of all goods, the TRUTH, arguments that could never end in compromise, regardless of how trifling the cause might be. The water coming out of our geyser was warm, I told her. Not hot, of course. But warm. Lukewarm, my mother responded. Come on, be sensible, it's lukewarm, almost cold. Warm, I said. Lying is bad: warm. We'll just see how far you get with your pig-headed stubbornness, said my mother, and now I knew how much a person had to want to wash as cold as was expected of them. Or at least pretend to do so. I got an idea of when lies are 'white lies' and therefore permitted, and I spent a week thinking how I might tell Herr Warsinsky that I too had a cold wash in the morning, as he'd thought. Tell him that we too had stood by the roadside when the Führer was to drive by.

Everyone is aware that we rarely feel the significance of events as they are happening, a fact that rarely causes us pain. That pain accompanied me throughout my childhood, and as it gradually abated and grew rarer, as the pain at the pain not occurring came more often, I grew up. In the cold lorry on that January morning, when I might have expected to encounter sharp pain as we passed the town's boundary, I remained cold, albeit also hopelessly unhappy at my coldness, something impossible to atone for. I remained cold as I heard my Auntie Alice, whom we called Lissy, break out in sobs, cold as I felt the deep breath that went through the lorry behind me, cold as I thought: If only they knew.

Children think that of adults almost every day. Yet I know full well when I first thought it, and it belongs to Sonnenplatz, which we could now no longer see, it belongs to crossing the town boundary and to that January morning, even though 'it' had happened eleven or twelve years earlier. I was being stubborn, I think, but I can't remember why. I may be foolish, I said to myself—or I felt it, for a four-year-old doesn't have words like that at her disposal, clumsy and awkward and bumping into everything and breaking everything—but I was not blind in my soul. Just as little as blindworms are blind, which I had heard tell slithered around in the Wepritz Hills, there where the known world ended and far away began. I couldn't understand how the people who were always talking about these blindworms had failed to notice that they never caught one, in fact never even seemed to see one. There was an obvious explanation and it testified not only to adults' unworldliness that they did not arrive at it: All these blindworms were enchanted princes and princesses, wearing crowns on their slim snakes' heads and calling, lisping with their forked tongues, for their likewise enchanted beloveds.

Oh dear God no, they weren't blind but they were invisible, and that was easy enough to understand, seeing as I too had a fierce desire for a magic cloak that would render me invisible to listen in as I wished to my parents' living-room conversations and to escape from bothersome people like the often-drunk tailor Herr Kopp from next door, but above all for my own soul to escape. Rid of its dull, heavy, disobedient body, my soul would be forced to float freely on mere air, and I would finally have the schadenfreude of seeing it as it was—a naked, pale, snaking worm, not unlike an appendix. There would be great excitement, everyone would come running to find the fleshy accoutrement to this shameless soul. I, however, would savour the wicked pleasure of denying my soul. In a voice of iron, I would commit the terrible sin of denying myself. No! I would say, repeating that no in the firmest of voices, abandoning the poor soul, that enchanted blindworm, to its fate, which I could not imagine being anything but bleak. While I myself, just like now, could sit outside the shop door in the mild afternoon sun and think wild, forbidden thoughts unpunished.

For then nothing in me would twitch when I lied, nothing would shrivel up in fear. Or convulse when I felt sorry for myself because I was a changeling child, like Foundling-Bird in the story, a child with no home, unloved despite all assertions and one day expelled, put outside locked doors in the wind. For that was how it was, there was no fooling me, or only for a short while when my mother came to my bedside, when she smiled just as convincingly as real mothers smile, when she had me fold my hands in prayer: I am small and pure of heart. My heart was not pure, though, but full of suspicion and full of dark wishes. How useful it would be, necessary and wise, to rid myself betimes of my own soul and be shot of it, so that I could look my mother in the eye in bed at night. And have you told me everything? You know you're to tell me everything every night at bedtime? Oh, to lie barefaced —Yes, everything, now and for ever!— and to know in secret: No, never again will I tell you everything. It's impossible.

I was shocked at myself, and that is the first shock I remember. I was shocked because I had asked myself: Who are you? And an answer came that wasn't a name any longer, but: Me.

And so I found out my fear was justified. Everyone and everything was ganging up on me and had forgotten all the hypocritical assurances from one moment to the next. I wasn't unprepared for them showing their true, unfamiliar faces—the dusty uncobbled road, the dirty yellow houses on the other side of it where my father's poorly paying customers lived, but also our own slightly better house behind my back, the back yard with the carpet-beating frame and the cellar stairs where the others gathered that day just as every other day, except without me. And even Sonnenplatz itself, nothing by the way but a sandy, sparsely vegetated empty space, had turned its back on me, no longer speaking to me.

It was terrible beyond all measure to be left in the lurch and singled out like that, but it was the consequence of having called myself 'me' in my innermost thoughts and being unable to stop repeating it: Me me me me me. Everything had to turn away from me; there was no other way. It was appalling, and it was just. I trembled with fear and guilt but also with bliss, all at the same time. I got up and was very proud.

And so life came towards me, a dark, shaggy beast, and once a person has seen it she is free in her decisions. You can of course go on as before. You can go inside when your mother calls you, but you indicate with a tiny smile that you might just as well stay outside and act the stranger, pretend to be Herr Rambow's daughter, for instance—a wicked, hideous thought that I burrowed my way into every night before I went to sleep.

Adults don't even notice when you spare them; they've forgotten that the possibilities of a person who calls herself 'me' then multiply, benign ones and terrifying ones. It was not yet determined which way I would one day turn. It was up to me to go on generously playing the good little child and savour the delight of obeying orders, or to be wicked and a changeling and to spread cares and woe around me like a squid spreads its cloud of ink in clear water. Over and over, I imagined how the parents of the frog prince must have felt when their lovely handsome good prince turned before their very eyes—surely not without his secret approval—into an ugly green frog. I, however, as I've said, preferred to think of the adorable blindworms.

There was no need to be told to keep silent about this, like with all important things. I was disappointed to note that everyone else did the same, as though they had all sat around a table at some point and made an agreement about what was to be spoken about in future and what not, under any circumstances. As ever, I had not been informed of these settlements and was left to find out the rules and their purpose for myself. I was very offended that the others didn't even seem to notice how far they moved away from their strict instructions never to lie and never to keep something a secret. I couldn't help adding every single lie and every single secret to the mountain of guilt growing inside me. With great relief, I turned to the evening prayer that Grandma Schnauzer sang to me in her reedy voice once, when I was allowed to spend the night with her in her big bed: Weary-eyed I go to re-hest. I was particularly fond of the second stanza: Wrong I may have done toda-hay, heed it not, dear God, I pra-hay. Father, may thy watchful ey-heye, guard the bed on which I lie-hie.

Yes, I said to my rear, into the lorry, we've already left the town, we're already in Wepritz, we're driving past the Lützen noodle factory. Oh, them! said my grandmother, they're long gone, you'll see. I'll bet they loaded up all their worldly goods and lugged them off to safety, that lot! And anyway, said my Auntie Alice, whom we called Lissy, the Lützens, they never knew how high to stick their noses in the air, am I right? But now, can they tie their noodle factory to a hot-air balloon and carry it away with them? Can they? No, nobody can, and it just goes to show—pride comes before a fall.

All seven of my adult relatives behind me in the lorry were very satisfied with that thought.

6

I won't claim that on that January day as we left our town behind us and then one place after another, like beads on a thread, the names of the towns and villages still familiar from Sunday excursions, and as the places became less known, despite the short distance we were able to travel—fifty kilometres, for our resting spot was the small town of Wriezen, on the other side, that is on this side of the River Oder; I won't claim that of all things that went through my mind it was the fire in the wicker chair in our nursery that came to me, the fire set by my brother Oddo at the age of six, whereupon my mother, who was fond of giving exaggerated names to simple events, perhaps to keep them from harming her very routine life at least through these dramatic names, called him an 'arsonist' several times over. It's even possible that this fire—the chair was old, my brother had tried to set the upholstery alight using several matches (Several! said my mother, appalled because that seemed to indicate the deliberate nature of the crime), but it only smoked and stank to high heaven—that this fire did not occur to me over all the years until today, as I ask myself how the complicated mechanism is laid out in us that we later call our 'conscience', why the memory of its first stirrings is lost to us and we only later notice it, once it has begun to work in the prescribed direction. The wicker-chair fire was treated, quite rightly we felt, like a capital crime.

In our family, where there were no strict rules and therefore no tendency for severe punishments, the decision over good and bad was in the hands of my mother, by dint of a moral superiority that was never questioned and was probably not granted by earthly powers. On the occasion of the wicker-chair fire, the needle veered very far towards 'bad'. Immediately after the successful, frantic extinguishing, immediately after it was clear that my brother, who had been at home alone, had not come to any harm (my mother repeated the words 'smoke poisoning', something I had never heard of before, in a kind of threatening delight), Oddo was dealt a pair of clips round the ear by our mother, which however did not yet count as punishment but as compensation for the shock he had given her, and as a solution to the conflict between concern for her son and outrage over his crime. Then she ordered herself: Don't hit him—as if I cared about that scruffy old wicker chair!

No one asked what she did care about, for that was obvious. A child, through his attempt to set his parental home alight, had professed a hostile relationship to that home. As there were no really serious matters at that time—we had been living in the new house for a year and were growing accustomed to it—this incident had to be treated as a serious matter. The boy had to be shown that his secret motives were clear, without stating those motives—not even to ourselves, for we didn't understand them. He had to be punished by ignoring him, and I, fearing nothing more than that punishment—deprived of our mother's gaze, not to mention her words, and, worst of all, her good-night kiss—I had to take part in the campaign, although no one asked it of me, although I had no schadenfreude this time, had no wish to demonstrate my good behaviour and no old score to settle with my brother—whom I must have loved, by the way, by all I know. From the depths of my criminal desires, I had to protect myself from myself by intensifying the punishment for him who had made my wishes reality. In the dark, however, behind my back, I held hot whispered conversations with my brother, conversations we had agreed in advance did not count. Yet the snake between our beds prevented us from coming together, as we usually did with no further ado when we were scared. We heard the snake's breathing when we held our breath, we heard the dead leaves covering its tree-trunk-thick body rustling, and we knew we mustn't move a muscle so as not to draw its serpentine attention.

On one of the next few days, my brother put his whole right hand on the glowing-hot electric hob in the kitchen, screamed to high heaven and my mother came running in her white shop coat, as usual in event of disaster without regard for any waiting customers. She dunked Oddo's hand in oil and she kissed every finger of the hand that had lit the fire, which was now coming out in blisters. She called him her little boy and rocked him on her lap, she blamed all of us for not looking after the child, she accused the shop, that accursed shop that hindered her from keeping her children unharmed, and she didn't even notice the happy expression emerging behind the tears on Oddo's face. Perhaps it was abhorrent to her for a moment that she had been forced to punish her son for a misdemeanour she was often so close to herself; but if there is a point to being an adult then it must be that one has learnt to keep to a strict, predetermined track in life and to strangle every thought of attempting to break out—and acts of desperation too are attempts to break out. If you knew how I was brought up! she'd say, but she never told us how she had been brought up. Except that they weren't allowed to make a sound at the table in their father's presence (which seemed ridiculous to us when we saw Grandpa Schnauzer at his kitchen table, making countless tiny cuts in the crust of his bread so that his toothless mouth could chew it. The way he could gurn and fold up his face when we asked him—Grandpa, fold your face in half!— so that we saw only the yellowed moustache dyed by snuff, and the way he sat quietly by the stove in his wicker chair for hours).

So that children don't have too hard a time 'in life', they shouldn't have it too easy 'in their youth'—which is therefore not life—that much was clear, once and for all. Once things got serious—in life, that is—the levity surely attached to them by a happy youth could only be a hindrance. At the same time it was important not to mingle these two phases—life and youth. You'll find out soon enough! we'd be told when we were ejected from the living room to enable the real conversations, the adult conversations. Once, I yanked the door back open and stuck my head back in the room, where they were still all sitting around the table, the air between them thick with confidentiality, and I said in the impudent tone that my mother sought to drive out of me more than anything else: I know what you're talking about anyway, you're talking about Auntie Magda's divorce! My mother followed me out into the hallway to tell me I had behaved extremely badly 'in front of everyone'. I had lost all joy in my naughtiness but I remained stubborn and made them beg me to set foot in the living room again.

Nobody, myself included, can say from where a child takes a desire for a life different to the good, right, firm life in which it is warmly and happily embedded, the way I was embedded in mine. I have a precise memory of the amazement when a girl joined our class, before the war, or at least before the major evacuations from the bombed-out cities. Her name was Inge and she came from Husum, and she declared outright that our town seemed ugly to her and she didn't understand how anyone could live there. She was very tall and slightly jittery in her movements, with crumbs stuck to her mouth after every meal. In my amazement I was not even offended, merely telling her I could never ever imagine having to live anywhere else. Since then I had observed myself, moving a chair to my window at the crack of dawn one Sunday to watch the sun going up and to test my sentiments when the first shudder of light fell across the town and the river and the fields beyond. That very same shudder went through me at the same moment; I told myself no other town, no other river could ever give me that feeling. Never again would I, as on that morning, feel such fear of the loss of a place, and at the same time that certainty that the loss was inescapable. If anything, then that fear and certainty explain my swift willingness to leave everything behind me once and for all on the morning we left, instead of ripping it out of me bit by bit. If anything, then this explains that trace of relief mingled with the utter tangle of sentiments as the lorry moved off.

A willingness that, on close consideration, was merely another form of fear—the fear that something unbearable might be expected of me. Although it is often confused with courage, by me as well, it gave me in any case a feeling of superiority over the others—a second singling out within the first that affected us all. And it was a trick that gave me ease, unlike the others who were tied to their wavering hope as if by ropes. For it was absolutely possible, probable even, they told each other beneath the tarpaulin on our lorry, that it would prove unnecessary to flee any further than Küstrin, that we would be caught up there—a phrase that was repeated over and over and very well determined and expressed our status as falling, plummeting individuals. That status, compared to the illusions of liberty and freedom we had all cherished previously, even in recent weeks, had something true to it. As though the great responsible party for everything that happened to us and others —the war—had at last decided in all its indifference not to beat about the bush any longer and to let us see in all openness, for it felt like that at this moment, what we really were in its eyes: nothing but dirt. That was not easily swallowed, of course, and I believe the moaning and groaning in the lorry gradually fell silent not only because one can't moan and groan without pause for ever but also because they found time to look around at each others' faces, which might resemble their own, and because they suddenly felt sharply that they could now, robbed of their possessions, no longer prove to anyone who they were. That is the only way to understand the never-ending talk by all refugees in the world of their abandoned possessions, their assertions, their exaggerations and unbearable bragging—if you listen to them, each one has left behind a knight's estate. As long as one talks of it, one as good as holds it in one's hand, and by forcing

another to take something—something lost,
ground to dust, shot to pieces, burnt to ash,
bombed to the ground or simply gambled away
through inadvertence—once again as whole and in
one piece and unlost for a few minutes, one forces
oneself to believe in place of the other.

At the time most of us were still embarrassed
when my Auntie Magda began to bemoan her
worldly goods. She said everything had been for
nothing, for no one could say she had got full use
out of a newly furnished apartment in only six
years. That was the time that had passed since her
divorce. Why 'newly furnished', said my Auntie
Alice, whom we called Lissy, in a mean tone of voice
—the furniture in her living room hadn't been new;
her husband, the filling-station owner Eberhard
Bieder in Schwerin, had been forced to hand it over
due to my father Bruno's persistence. What do you
mean by hand it over, said Auntie Magda, Eberhard
behaved like a gentleman, always, nobody can say
otherwise, and I didn't mean the living-room furniture, I meant all the other furniture. To think of
my brand-new kitchen! All for nothing! No one felt
comfortable with the way she said in such barefaced terms that their life, now irrevocably behind
them, could creep into a kitchen cupboard or a
twelve-piece collector's set of cups. Auntie Magda

was referred to in the family as 'far too good', with a slight undertone of contempt for an unworldliness bordering on stupidity. My mother used to say Auntie Magda—my father's youngest sister—was a 'chattering Nancy'. She chattered her way through life, she said, and Auntie Magda, who was kind and friendly to everyone, was particularly friendly with my mother because she was afraid of her superiority. She downplayed herself and called my mother 'Charlottchen', Little Charlotte, but drew her lips slightly inwards as she said it. Even then, in the manner of people whose true lives are in the past, she carried a wallet full of photos with her, foisting them on everyone who crossed her path. She held the person by the arm as she explained her pictures, all of them showing her far-off wonderful days with her unfaithful but gentlemanly husband, on whom she had probably foisted photos from her youth with that same grip on his arm. I too had learnt early on to react with a touch of condescension to the friendly gestures and gifts from Auntie Magda, who called me her darling as loudly as she could. I saw her snapping up a friendly or complimentary word with her darting brown eyes, like a treat to be digested without shame in plain view, and relentlessly trying to buy such emotional treats with gifts and favours, because the world otherwise

seemed too cold and hostile for her childish dispo-
sition. For her, the whole world was populated by
'nice people', the sole exception being that redheaded madam who had found a way to sneak into
her husband Eberhard's affections, he being a weak
but otherwise fine and even gentlemanly person.

My first exercise in self-control consisted of
leaving a box of chocolates given to me by Auntie
Magda untouched in my cupboard for a week. The
feeling of cloying sweetness and gluttony that her
visit left behind would have risen to exorbitant,
unpermitted levels had I eaten the chocolates as
well. People do have to know how to control themselves, said my mother once Auntie Magda had
gone, and she didn't mean any individual lack of
control that her sister-in-law had been guilty of but
her entire being that overflowed in all directions.
And so I decided not to eat the chocolates and
informed my brother Oddo, who didn't understand
my decision but admired it and was immediately
prepared to monitor it by checking on the chocolate box every day and support it by voluntarily
going without sweets in my presence.

There were exercises for which I needed my
brother for comparison—who can hold their breath
the longest, who can stay silent the longest, who can
be tickled without laughing, who can extinguish a

candle between forefinger and thumb and who can stand to spend at least five minutes in the absolute dark of the evening basement. A prolonged need for self-punishment must have driven me on, and I wonder what forbidden pleasures I had to castigate myself for. My mother had an extremely contemptuous way of calling someone a 'pleasure seeker'. Oh him! she'd say with something approaching disgust, he's a pleasure seeker!—explaining or considering possible the unfortunate person's every misdemeanour. You don't want to be a pleasure seeker, do you? she'd ask me when she caught me eating sweets. This caused an unholy compulsion to eat sweets, and I developed a technique for brushing past the relevant boxes in the shop, in which loose confectionary was offered under transparent cellophane, sorted by quality, and helping myself to a handful, to begin with the cheaper sorts and later only the most expensive. I knew I would never admit to this theft, and I prepared myself for tenacious lies, which horrified me almost more than the theft itself, although in reality it was never necessary because the confectionary was never missed and I was never asked about it. I grew bold and took tins of sweet, thick condensed milk, stirring cocoa powder into it. I sat down by the window looking out onto Soldiner Strasse, spooned the milk and read something I was forbidden to read: Lessing's *Emilia Galotti* or the *Schwarzes Korps* SS newspaper, which my mother kept out of reach of us children just like the two volumes of *The Human Body*, which contained fold-out diagrams of the body with all its organs, male and female, and certain keywords under which information was to be found. And so that information is forever linked for me with the taste of sweet condensed milk and the smell of moth powder, for the *Human Body* books were kept in my parents' wardrobe beneath the mothballed winter clothing and emanated the scent of moth powder whenever I turned the pages. I had sometimes seen a volume on my father's bedside table, in earlier times, when we came to his bed for 'rough and tumble' on Sunday mornings. That meant we took turns sitting on his drawn-up knees and he had to try to throw us off.

The cycle of guilt-confession-punishment-repentance was so deeply etched on my innermost sense of necessity and balance that I had to take over punishment and atonement myself whenever I managed to eliminate external justice. That was when I began my exercises in emotional hardening, for a weak person was almost as much at risk as a pleasure seeker, and anyone who was afraid was weak. I was afraid, though, and I knew too that fear, as terrible as it was, also has something pleasurable, ticklish about it, as long as one can succumb to it without restriction and as long as every attack of fear comes before hope for comfort and salvation. When my brother and I still shared our nursery on Sonnenplatz and he still slept in his cot, three years old at most, I woke one morning and saw a hooded man leaning over his bed in the grainy light. At that instant, I grew certain that the man was holding a knife and wanted to stab my little Oddo. I heard our parents getting ready outside, I saw the comforting strip of light beneath the door, but the bright hall-way was almost unreachable for me because I'd have to creep past the hooded man. Even so, I couldn't make myself guilty of my brother's death. So I crept on tiptoe in terrible fear past his back, yanked the door open and reported to my mother, combing her hair in her petticoat in the bathroom, that someone wanted to stab Oddo. My brave mother immediately followed me into the nursery and laughed as she showed me the murderer, now bathed in light: the pile of clothes on the chair next to my brother's bed, which from behind had the outline of a shapeless, bending hooded man. I don't know why I still couldn't calm down, why I called for my mother again to ask her to move the clothes so they'd lose their ominous shape.

That was a fear I liked remembering, and there were also fears that found their absolute, liberating resolution through the regular, orderly process of guilt-fear-punishment-atonement-forgiveness. When I was seven and my brother almost four, we would fight mercilessly for the slightest reason. I think we had built a system of corridors and dungeons on the floor out of wooden blocks, in which our most beautiful marble, a cat's eye with a rainbow-coloured twist, was to be held prisoner as an enchanted prince. We ended up arguing over the best way to guard the prince; I was in favour of maximum severity with no meals but my brother wanted to smuggle food in for him secretly and got into a terrible rage when my marble guards thwarted his attempt. At the time he had fits of temper that we all feared; Bodo has a temper on him, said my mother, amazed that one of her children should have such a flaw. So Oddo lost his temper, stamping his feet and yelling his head off, and for the first time one of his gestures made me suspect that this fit might be a drama, acted out to get his own way, and I felt deceived. I was seized by rage and we grappled bitterly, rolling on the floor, destroying our prison system, panting and trying to hurt each other. All at once he cried out—the cry was real, ran icy down my spine—and lay still and weeping. He couldn't move his right arm. I dragged him to our bed, sat him at the head end, wrapped him up in soft covers like a sweating cure, squatted down at the tail end of the bed and promised him everything I owned if he'd only make his arm better. He merely went on crying, his face swelling up, and said he couldn't just do that, he couldn't. That was how our mother found us, and as usual in difficult situations she immediately did what was needed, wasting little time on questions and scolding but calling the doctor and unceremoniously cutting the sweater and shirt off my brother, whose arm had swollen up in the meantime. This waste made a mighty impression on me and reinforced my conviction that I had committed a crime for which I could never atone. I stood at the foot of the chaise longue in the living room, wringing my hands. My mother came in and patted me hard on the shoulder, saying only: There, see what damage you can do! I told her not to smack me and she didn't because I wasn't at all important to her; the only important one was Oddo, whom the doctor took in his car straight to hospital, where fortunately a gallant young doctor, whom I imagined as incredibly handsome and brave, managed to reset the arm from its very complicated dislocation. It could have stayed stiff, my mother said when she got home that afternoon, it was such a complicated injury—she had a liking for the word 'complicated'. In any case, my brother had been kept in hospital and there were only three of us that evening. I was sent to bed early and my parents laid out our dinner on the round table in my bedroom. My mother brought my plate to my bed, nicely garnished as she usually only did when we had visitors. All three of us were so relieved that my brother had been saved; we laughed together and I, with my penchant for formulations, told myself in all earnest before I went to sleep: This has been one of the happiest evenings in my life.

I am certain that many a proud stance, much heroism in hopeless situations, but also much exaggerated fear and cowardice come from a strong awareness of humiliation. I, for example, as I have said, possessed that awareness and I wish I knew where it came from. My earliest memories lead me to incidents in which justice was violated, always leaving me with a feeling of irreparable damage to the world's order and of my own humiliation through impotence. The settings of such incidents that incurred that feeling only occur to me as their background, a landscape, a road, a room. As indicative as it may be that my brother's birth and infancy have left almost no trace on my memory, my first recollection of him is just as revealing, linked as it is to an injustice dealt to him—a slap from my mother for an allegedly wet nappy that proved on closer inspection to be dry. The scolding for the rubber pants said to have caused the mistake did not of course redeem the injustice done to my brother. In fact, any injustice suffered seemed to be irredeemable, perhaps the reason why I tried so hard not to draw injustice upon myself. When it did happen, however, if someone had the misfortune of injuring me, it was easy enough for me to forgive the causer of that injustice, even carry on loving that person, but I never forgot the injustice done to me. I never forgot the shove given to me by my very first friend, Lieselotte, the daughter of Herr Kurth the tailor from the house next door on Sonnenplatz. I knew that Herr Kurth was a drinker and that the Kurths bought things 'on the slate' in my father's black book. I sensed a deep reason behind his sad zigzagging gait and his melancholy repetition of the same song: You can't be true to me, no no, oh no you can't, though your lips say you're true, I know that you aren't. I laughed at the time like the others when Lieselotte, who had slightly protruding brown eyes and a hard hazelnut head with two stiff plaits, dragged her father into the house by the hand. I always hid when I could, understanding that this scene ought not to have witnesses. Once, though, I was playing on my scooter right in front of her door and couldn't get away quickly enough. Her father was heading straight for me; Lieselotte pulled me away and shoved me so hard I fell over. Your heart has many lovers, sang Herr Kurth. His smaller children and his wife were watching his arrival from behind the starched white kitchen curtain and the potted Busy Lizzies, which always blossomed like crazy in the Kurths' house, and I dusted down my playsuit. Yet for me there is no other, sang Herr Kurth. Lieselotte was ashamed and I realized our friendship was over—an injustice through no fault of my own. I ran to the Gewoba Gang, who were playing in the sandy hollows on unkempt Sonnenplatz, and let them all ride on my scooter, not caring a bit if they ruined it. I was wild for their friendship, showing them against the wall that I could beat every one of them at Sevens, having practised throwing and catching the ball indefatigably over the past weeks. They had to let me pick the next game. Who's afraid of the bogeyman? No one! I yelled at the top of my voice like all the others, and was terribly afraid. Here he comes in his big black car! yelled Erwin, Police Constable Baldin's older son, the head of the Gewoba Gang. We'll go to

A-mer-i-ca! we shouted, the bogeyman now at
our backs but the never-ending ocean ahead of us.
A-mer-i-ca's all burnt away! triumphed Erwin, and
I, smaller than them all, shouted the loudest: We'll
get over a-ny-way! I did get over, reaching burnt-
down America ten times over and winning and now
finally allowed to play hide and seek with them, 'in
all the yards', as the phrase went, expressing no
more and no less than that the entirety of the
Gewoba Buildings complex was transformed in a
single instant into a foreign continent because we
now roamed the courtyards, just as innocent and
bare and draught-ridden as they ever were, but with
us now hunters or the hunted, everything that
could offer no hiding place or safety now indifferent
and invisible. Helmut Baldin, who was the same
age as me and was also allowed to play for the first
time, was caught cheating. He peeped through his
fingers as he stood with his face against the carpet-
beating frame and counted to a hundred so that we
could hide. His brother Erwin ruled that the round
didn't count, and Helmut let his fists and feet loose
on him and then on all of us, and Erwin wanted
to get rid of the kid once and for all by sending me
to his father with the message: Helmut's making
trouble. I planted myself outside our building and
called up this message, impossible to rebel against,

of course, to Police Constable Baldin on the second floor. He leant out of the window in a white vest and braces, his uniform jacket no doubt on a hook in the corridor, but he was still a police constable and his instruction to bring Helmut to him was tantamount to an order. I was prevented from carrying it out by my mother, however, who called me inside with an expression betiding calamity and gave me my first and only beating. Don't be a tell-tale tit, were her embittered words. Where did you get that from? I felt I was in the process of spoiling and that perhaps telling tales was the beginning of the road, at the end of which a person was condemned to lurch around in a zigzag in front of everyone and sing: You can't be true to me . . .

That was around the time I began training ladybirds, which could be caught in their reams around Sonnenplatz and in the Wepritz Hills. I shut them up in matchboxes and forced them to follow special paths I had dug for them in the sand. For disobedience, they were blocked into dark sand caves from which they tried to crawl out again and again. I got great pleasure out of pressing them back into the loose sand, and I have since known something about the origins of childhood cruelty. It can be no coincidence that I referred to myself as their 'teacher', that I planted gardens of gorse and heather for them, in which they were allowed to wander at leisure once they had obediently walked my paths. The only thing they were never allowed was to fly away without my permission.

My first teacher, Herr Warsinsky, was a gentle but sometimes unexpectedly unjust and quick-tempered man, who had nothing against grabbing two girls by their plaits and banging their heads together—a procedure to which my former friend Lieselotte's hazelnut head provoked him in particular. I told myself I would die if he did such a thing to me, and I began to struggle for safety from his temper by obtaining his affection. I didn't find school difficult but it was hard for me to overcome my shyness and make it clear to Herr Warsinsky that I was a good student. I was very clumsy and he, as though he had seen through my plan and had no intention of making it easier for me, missed no opportunity to ridicule me. And then he praised me for something that was not of my doing, which I knew next to nothing about and which I would have otherwise hidden from everyone out of embarrassment. He announced that my mother had given some of my used clothes to a certain Gerda, who was also in my class and lived close to us with her parents, in a flat where 'incredible conditions' prevailed, as my mother informed us. I was unhappy at his sudden outbreak of friendliness, feeling perfectly well that it was not directed at me but at people who had something to give away in general. Gerda, whom I hadn't cared about either way beforehand, became most abhorrent to me and it was one of my worst chores when my mother told me to take something to Gerda's family, food or clothing.

Herr Warsinsky, meanwhile, returned to his old dislike of me, I could tell quite clearly, when I came back from a special holiday on the Baltic, which my mother had obtained on my behalf through a highly exaggerated doctor's certificate presented to the headmaster. When Herr Warsinsky began to quiz me on my first day back on things I couldn't possibly have learnt and I, frozen in the face of such injustice, maintained a stubborn silence even at easy questions, he finally exclaimed that I must still have my bathing cap over my brain!

I saw I would have to go to special effort to win over Herr Warsinsky, a mission dear to my heart, for really I adored him by that point, lapping up his every word when he told us about the Führer's path of great sacrifice and when he described Jesus Christ as a forerunner to the Führer. He came to school in SA uniform on the movement's commemorative dates, he stretched his chubby body up straight when we sang *Die Fahne hoch!* and his saluting arm seemed never to waver, as mine sadly did when the national anthem followed on from that song of the movement. He said anyone who couldn't even hold their arm up for that long was a weakling, and we were to imagine what the movement's martyrs had been through and should jolly well toughen up. Upon which I stood in our living room every day, sang the Horst Wessel song and the national anthem three times in a row and forced myself not to lower my arm, no matter how numb it grew, no matter how much it trembled afterwards. At the next flag ceremony, however, the teacher didn't even notice my steadfastness.

And then we found out, how I no longer know, that Herr Warsinsky's birthday was on the twenty-fourth of September. I seized the opportunity, put the fairy tale 'King Thrushbeard' into rough verses and secretly memorized it with the whole class after school. On the twenty-fourth of September, we all took flowers to school. My grandmother had taken my bunch of asters away from me and cut a new bouquet from our garden. 'A flower without leaves is for a man with no honour!' she said. We strung a line across the classroom and placed blankets over it as our curtain. Herr Warsinsky was most surprised when we presented our programme and congratulated him on his birthday, which, however, was not on that day at all but on a date during the summer holidays. Yet he proved himself equal to our great goodwill, recognized me as the originator and put his arm around my shoulders, and since that day I had no need to fear INJUSTICE from him. My friend Hella and I always brought him flowers on the twenty-fourthth of September even long after we changed schools. Every time, he would put his arm around us and say to his wife: These are my most loyal students.

It had emerged that I could write poems. One day I dared, instead of an essay on the ninth of November, the date of the November betrayal and the stab in the back, to hand in a poem. It began with the lines:

> Surrounded by enemies on all sides
> Our land was in great danger.
> But German soldiers brave and true
> Let in not a single stranger.
>
> Vile betrayal by the Jews
> Made Germany plea defeat.
> But Germany moved on swiftly,
> Despite war damage most replete.

Herr Warsinsky, initially unwilling to believe I had written the poem myself and not copied it out of the newspaper, came close to my desk and inspected me in surprise. Then he said I was 'a devil of a fellow'.

My first major conscious lie is also linked to him. I had brought a cork into school, a toy painted all over with my paint set and stuck with tiny brass nails, something I had made at home and was extremely proud of. I showed it off in the break, it passed from hand to hand, and by the next lesson began I hadn't got it back. Instead, Herr Warsinsky spotted it, being played with by a girl in the last row of desks. He took it away from her; she protested because it didn't belong to her. When he asked whose it was, she named me. This is yours? asked Herr Warsinsky. I thought he was immeasurably disappointed that I would waste my time on such nonsense, and denied it. No, it's not my cork! Everyone testified against me, all knowing I had brought it in with me. Gundel, who sat next to me and whom I'd have given anything to be friends with, looked aghast at me and shifted away. I knew, though, that there was no going back. I clenched my teeth and felt myself plummet into bottomless depravity, denied and denied and asked myself how I should ever find my way back into the company of decent, truth-telling people. But I denied.

Well, said Herr Warsinsky, even if it's not yours, do you want it anyway?

No, I said, horrified. What would I want with a thing like that?

7

I never visited the Seelow Hills again. They are probably harmless but on that late afternoon, in the impending darkness, amid drifting snow, black ice and great cold, they were an almost unconquerable hindrance. We leapt from our places and pushed, sliding on the icy smooth ground ourselves.

The second Hannemann lorry was tethered in front of ours—we absolutely had to scale this mountain range for the first time. Still incredulous and weakened like at a dress rehearsal, we experienced the harried fear of people who had to reach an absurd goal at all cost. We were on the other side of the Oder, we had crossed the bridge, so we had surely acquired the right once again to be defended by the soldiers, for whom the frozen river at least offered natural assistance. The soldier who had perched for so long on the shaft between our lorry and the trailer behind it and had rather belonged to us since my brother had almost tipped over his head the contents of the bucket that was passed around in our lorry when one of the children or older people had to relieve themselves—that soldier had suddenly disappeared from my side. I could thus answer no to the military policemen who approached us at that moment and inspected us quickly but thoroughly, when they asked whether there were any Wehrmacht members among us. Our convoy moved off, the wheels now wrapped about with chains, and the Seelow Hills were not unconquerable; we held tight to our lorry and were pulled up along with it. If the soldier hadn't skedaddled in time, I thought, would I have had to report him to the watchdogs? They would have lugged him up by the armpits and dragged him along between them. I could see his face, to which I had paid no previous attention, but now it jerked around to me; I retained his incredulous expression for ever.